Fear crashed through Danielle's stomach, nearly stealing her breath.

Yet for the first time in well over a year, she wasn't alone. She had someone she could ask for help. But she wasn't very good at doing that, either.

God, if it's safe to let Nate in, please show me.

It seemed that the more she prayed for peace, the more her life spun out of control. The spying eyes. The jimmied lock. The butterflies that Nate caused.

She'd come to Crescent City to run away from her father's death. But she hadn't counted on a whole new set of problems.

Nate was nearly to his car, and she had to make a decision.

"Wait!" She jogged over to him. "On Tuesday I thought someone was following me home. I'm afraid they might try again tonight." His face turned stony. "Would you mind just following me to make sure no one else is behind me?"

She'd barely closed her mouth before he agreed. "I'll be right behind you."

Books by Liz Johnson

Love Inspired Suspense

The Kidnapping of Kenzie Thorn
Vanishing Act

LIZ JOHNSON

After graduating from Northern Arizona University in Flagstaff with a degree in public relations, Liz Johnson set out to work in the Christian publishing industry, which was her lifelong dream. In 2006 she got her wish when she accepted a publicity position at a major trade book publisher. While working as a publicist in the industry, she decided to pursue her other dream—being an author. Along the way to having her novel published, she wrote articles for several magazines.

Liz lives in Colorado Springs, Colorado, where she enjoys theater, ice skating, volunteering in her church's bookstore and making frequent trips to Arizona to dote on her nephew and three nieces. She loves stories of true love with happy endings. Visit her online at www.lizjohnsonbooks.com.

Liz Johnson
VANISHING ACT

Steeple
Hill®

Published by Steeple Hill Books™

STEEPLE HILL BOOKS

Steeple
Hill®

Recycling programs
for this product may
not exist in your area.

ISBN-13: 978-0-373-67427-5

VANISHING ACT

Copyright © 2010 by Elizabeth Johnson

Printed in U.S.A.

"For God has not given us a spirit of fear and timidity, but of power, love, and self-discipline."
—*2 Timothy* 1:7

To Julia, Rachel, Caleb, Emily, and Jacob,
I count myself blessed beyond measure
to be your aunt. May our family leave a legacy
that you are proud to carry on, one of grace,
hope and love.

PROLOGUE

A car parked at least a block away backfired loudly, making Nora James huddle against the car door. Alone inside the car, she wrapped her arms around her stomach and leaned closer to the tinted window of the Lincoln Town Car, searching for any sign of the events unfolding in the dark alley. But night surrounded the car, cloaking the men she knew lined the brick buildings on each side of the narrow street.

Twisting her long ponytail behind her shoulder, she pressed her ear against the window, hoping for a voice she recognized. Cars sped over the bridge, crossing the nearby Willamette River, but everything else was silent.

No birds chirping. No people talking or strolling along the river. Not even the soft tinkling of evening rain, strange for the time of year. Eerily silent.

Suddenly the door on the opposite side of the bench seat jerked open, and a large man filled the opening. The car's dome light spread an ethe-real glow over his menacing sneer. His shoulders stretched his Italian suit jacket, and his hair was slicked back with something the consistency of motor oil. He made an imposing figure, but Nora was surprisingly glad to see a face that she recognized.

It was neither friendly nor safe, but it was familiar. And she had dearly missed anything familiar since being forced into a nondescript, white van three days earlier.

It had all been so cliché. Walking to the home that she shared with her dad from her final class of the day, she had lifted her face to the warmth of the sun, a rarity in the usually cloudy Portland climate. Lost in thoughts of her upcoming college graduation, she'd ignored the world around her.

That day it had been far from silent. Couples walking down the sidewalk, chatting vibrantly to each other. Cars flying by. The subdued chime of bicycle bells.

But then the world tilted on its axis. The screeching tires of the white van immediately signaled that something was amiss, and the men who jumped from the open sliding door moved like lightning. Both linebacker types and dressed in black, they easily subdued Nora, throwing her onto the floor of the van and slamming the door closed as the vehicle jerked forward.

For three days her life had consisted of a dark room, a flat mattress on a cement floor and the man who now leaned in toward her. Lurch. At least, that's what she'd nicknamed him in her mind the first time he brought her a glass of water. He didn't really resemble the character from one of her favorite childhood television shows, but when she and her dad started watching the old reruns together, the original Lurch had frightened her, too.

"Ms. James?" Lurch asked quietly in the same voice he always used with her.

"Yes?"

He cleared his throat, covering his mouth with his hand. His bushy, brown eyebrows pinched together, not unlike an expression her academic advisor frequently made.

Involuntarily she leaned a little bit closer to him, willing him to tell her what was going on. In three days no one had uttered a word about why she had been taken. No one said anything about where she was or what they intended to do to her. Or why they needed her alive.

She'd decided on the first day that if they didn't need her alive, they would have taken her out of the picture.

Immediately.

The men she glimpsed were hard, with glowering faces and wicked-looking weapons. The kind of men who dispatched unwanted, unneeded women without a second thought.

"It's going to be a few more minutes," Lurch interrupted her thoughts. "He's not here yet."

"Who? Who are we waiting for?"

Lurch looked confused but didn't answer as he closed the door behind him.

And Nora was plunged into darkness again.

Her head spun and her eyes watered. She felt drugged.

Maybe she was drugged.

"God, a little help here, please?" she pleaded. "I know I haven't been praying nearly as I much as I should, but I have been a little distracted with trying to escape. Of course, You know all this. And You know what's going on outside, and I sure don't." She sighed. "So whatever happens, could You take care of me? And Dad, too. Please don't let him worry about me too much." A bit of a futile prayer, as her dad was a world-class worrier, but it never hurt to ask.

Just then headlights flashed into the alley, splashing light along the brick buildings then illuminating the interior of the Town Car. Nora blinked against the brightness, holding her forearm up to her eyes.

A door from the other car slammed, but the lights stayed on.

"Where is she?" demanded a voice she'd know anywhere.

She yanked on the handle, pushing hard on the door, trying again to open it without luck. "Dad! I'm in here! Can you hear me?" she screamed into the window. "Dad! I'm right here!"

"Nora! Nora, I'm here!"

She slammed into the door again. "Dad! I'm in the car!"

A silky voice called out, "Enough."

When he spoke again, her father's voice sounded as though he had turned to face the far side of the alley. "Goodwill, I'm here. Let her go." Her dad's voice was stronger than usual, out of character for the quiet accountant.

She could almost picture him in his green sweater-vest and white, collared shirt. The last time she'd seen him, he was wearing a hideous orange tie under the vest, and his hair was in complete disarray, brown spikes sticking up all over. Her father certainly didn't have the best fashion sense, but she couldn't love him more if he dressed like David Beckham.

Nora pounded her fist once against the window again, the knock echoing inside the car, then stopped when she realized the conversation in the alley disappeared beneath the sound. She'd never be able to hear her father's voice if she kept banging. Sagging against the door, she once more strained to hear the voices on the other side.

"Good evening, Parker. So glad you could join us." That voice was deep and smooth as satin. Its very sound seemed to vibrate the windows, making Nora pull back slightly from her position hovering over the door handle.

"Goodwill, I'm the one that you want. Let Nora go. Please." Her father's voice shook on the last word. Something she'd never heard before.

"Not until I get what I want."

"Fine! I'll do it. I'll take care of everything. No one will be able to trace the money back to you. But this is the last time. No more."

What was her dad talking about? Was he laundering money for the men who kidnapped her? Why would he put them both in danger like this?

"I'll decide when you're finished."

"No—" her dad began.

"I think I've proven that you don't want to be on my bad side. Do what I say and you and your daughter are safe. Don't, and you'll see what a mess that can be." Goodwill said something more, but he must have turned away because his voice was muffled. She couldn't make out a word of it.

Suddenly the car door, which had been her support, jerked open and one of Lurch's comrades grabbed her upper arm, yanking her to her feet.

Nora stumbled, gasped, then gagged on the awful stench that filled the alley. Moonlight illuminated rows of Dumpsters overflowing with rotting food particles and what smelled like animal waste.

She covered her nose and mouth with her free hand as the thug jerked her toward the front of the car and into the stream of light.

And there was her father, looking battered and emotionally bruised. Purple shadows swelled beneath his eyes and his cheeks sunk into his mouth. Bloodshot eyes swept eagerly over her from head to toe, certainly searching for any injuries.

"Dad, are you okay?" she asked, disappointed when her voice came out a scratchy whisper.

"I'm fine. I'm just so sorry that I got us mixed up in this."

Barely three feet away from him, Nora could stand the distance no longer and lunged at him, ripping her arm from her captor's hand and throwing herself into her father's waiting embrace. He held her close and smoothed her matted, blond hair down her shoulders.

"Well, isn't this reunion sweet?" The words dripped with sarcasm, and Nora had no doubt that they came from the man her father had called Goodwill. She had yet to actually set eyes on the man, but her father squeezed her closer, impeding her attempt to turn and face the menacing man.

"Listen to me closely, Nora," he whispered into

her ear so low that she had to strain to make out the words. "I don't think this is going to go the way that I want it to. If something happens to me, I want you to get out of here. Go to the apartment and get the money that's stashed in my sock drawer and—"

"But, Dad. I won't leave you."

"Yes, you will." His voice was low and fierce, almost a growl. "Get the money and get out of town. Get rid of your cell phone and don't leave any traces. You'll never be safe here. Please just go."

"But how will you find me?"

"I won't."

Tears sprang to her eyes as her father pushed her away, stepping toward the two men behind her.

One of the men was Lurch. The other she'd never seen before. He was immensely attractive with features so handsome they bordered on beautiful. Graceful cheekbones that flowed into a round chin. Perfectly arched nose. Every strand of blond hair perfectly gelled into place and piercing blue eyes as cold as ice. His gaze locked on to Nora's as she took an involuntary step back.

"I trust my staff has kept you comfortable, Ms. James." His voice as smooth as his appearance, Nora was certain that she was being addressed by Goodwill, but she still had no idea who he was.

Other than that he had obviously had her kidnapped.

"I'm here. I'll do whatever you want. Now let Nora go," her dad said in a quiet yet firm tone.

Goodwill put his finger on his chin and tapped it as though deep in thought, but his eyes remained cold. Hard. "I think not yet. After all, we'll need a little leverage if you decided to suddenly change your mind. What if you decided to turn state's evidence? What kind of businessman would I be if I had already let my leverage go. No, the girl stays with us until the job is done."

"No!" Her dad lunged forward, his hands balled into fists, his entire body shaking wildly. He seemed childlike in size compared to Goodwill, but he held nothing back as he slammed into the other man. Goodwill barely shuffled his feet at the impact, then stepped to the side as the flailing man stumbled to the ground.

Suddenly the thug, who had pulled Nora from the car, appeared at Goodwill's side, aiming a large black gun at her father. Her dad's face fell as he stared up at the barrel.

"Don't!" she cried, taking a quick step toward the trio, stopping only when the gun suddenly swiveled and leveled directly at her chest.

"I think it would be wise for you stay put." Goodwill's voice was like iron.

Nora looked into the tortured face of her father.

"I'm so sorry, Baby," he whispered. Still leaning on the ground, his weight supported by one elbow, he said very clearly, "I wonder why there's no rain tonight."

The commotion was immediate. Goodwill shouted, "Check him for a bug!" The oaf with the gun kicked her dad in the stomach, and he grunted loudly. Suddenly the gun exploded, the flash from the muzzle surprisingly brilliant in the darkness of the alley, illuminating the red stain immediately seeping into his sweater vest.

Nora dove behind the open door of her dad's car, landing half on the driver's seat and smashing one knee into the dashboard.

"Get the girl!" Goodwill roared. The goon did as he was told, running toward her.

She had no time to think about her actions, and moved purely out of self-preservation. She turned the keys, sending up a prayer of thankfulness that he'd left them in the ignition. Yanking her other leg into the car, she shifted into Reverse and punched the accelerator. The old sedan, one door still open, flew down the alley away from the man with the gun. Away from the stream of Goodwill's curses.

Away from her father's lifeless body.

She rammed into a large, metal Dumpster before yanking the steering wheel and spinning around to drive forward. A quick glance in the rearview mirror was all she managed before her back windshield shattered with a crack.

She ducked low, keeping her foot on the gas.

ONE

Eighteen months later

Nathan Andersen needed a nap. Badly.

He yawned for the millionth time, fighting eyelids that threatened to close even as his car swerved down the highway at midnight. A sudden tremor against his leg nearly sent him through the roof, and he dove into his pocket for his cell phone.

"Agent Andersen."

"Hey, Boss."

"Someone's burning the midnight oil," he said, chuckling. "Have you left the office yet, Heather?"

Her long pause answered his question. "You asked me to call if we heard anything else from Roth about Nora and your assignment."

"Yes. What'd he say? Did he overhear another phone call with more details?" The FBI mole's first tip was trusted enough to put Nate on the road to Crescent City. What he learned next could make or break the assignment.

"Not exactly. It was more of a confirmation of what he already told us. Roth said that he heard Goodwill—" whose lawyer had gotten him out on bail a couple months before "—on the phone with the Shadow." Both agents remained silent for a moment. For years the Shadow's name meant nothing but disappointment to the FBI. He was probably the best assassin in recent history, and the file on him was filled only with death certificates of his victims.

No names—pseudonyms or real. No pictures. No physical description. No location. Nothing to help them find him.

Heather cleared her throat and continued. "Roth said that he heard Goodwill confirming with the Shadow that he arrived in Crescent City and he was sure that Nora James was there. He said something about the community college, but Roth wasn't sure what was going on."

Nate's breathing quickened. He had to find her first, or it could spell the end of their case. "Did he say if the plan had changed?"

"Roth didn't hear anything about a change. As far as we know, the idea is still for the Shadow to kidnap Nora and hold her until Goodwill's trial is over. What are you going to do?"

Nate grunted. "If Goodwill's plan hasn't changed,

then neither has mine." Another jaw-stretching yawn caught him off guard, and he mumbled an apology. Hitting the speaker button on his phone, he tossed it into the center console. Using his now-free hand to search for something that might help him fight off sleep, he grabbed for the coffee cup sitting next to his phone. Scowling when he realized it was empty, he chucked it at the opposite floorboard and rooted around the passenger seat for the bag of sunflower seeds he'd stashed there hours earlier.

"Do you really think Nora is in Crescent City?" Heather sounded unconvinced. "I know Roth doesn't have any reason to mislead us, but she took off a year and half ago. She could be anywhere by now. How can we be sure Goodwill tracked her to a tiny little town no one's ever heard of?"

Nate shoved a handful of seeds into his mouth and tried to talk around them. "I don't know how he found her, but he's got no reason to lie to Roth about hiring the Shadow to kidnap her and hold her as blackmail again. Goodwill will do anything to stay out of jail and he knows the evidence we have against him could put him away for life."

Red taillights flashed down the road, sending Nate back to the night in the alley that his years of investigation into Phil Goodwill's crime syndicate had led to. That night hadn't ended well, especially when Parker James, Nate's key witness and the master of Goodwill's perfectly manufactured monetary fronts had been shot.

His arm twitched, jerking him back to the present at the same time that Heather asked, "Do you really think that Goodwill will try to kidnap Nora again? Especially since she didn't know anything about her father's involvement with the crime ring?"

Nate laughed out loud. "You'd think he'd have learned his lesson last time. In seven years with the Bureau, I've never seen anyone turn as fast as Parker did when his daughter was kidnapped. He couldn't wait to turn over state's evidence to get Goodwill behind bars. He practically taped that wire on himself before going into the alley."

Nate shook his head at the memory of the agitated and jerky accountant so focused on rescuing his daughter. Now Nate had a job to do. One that could clinch his case against one of the biggest criminals in the Portland area. He couldn't afford to let the guy back out on the street for good.

And to keep that from happening, he had to focus on his two witnesses. Both in danger. One in immediate peril.

"Will you keep an eye on the old man while I'm out of town? Just check in on him from time to time."

"Sure thing, Boss. Is there anything I should tell him?"

Nate chewed on his lip for a moment, instinctively reaching for the coffee cup before remembering it was empty. "Don't tell him I'm going after Nora. He doesn't need to know that Goodwill's last-ditch plan for freedom is kidnapping his daughter. Again."

"Okay."

"I don't want Parker even thinking that he might not testify at the trial. His testimony rounds out this case perfectly. I'll find Nora and get her to the safe house. I won't let Goodwill intimidate the old man by threatening Nora."

Heather yawned loudly on the other end of the line. "Oh, sorry. Guess it's getting late here, too." Her definition of late was a little different than his.

"Go home—get some rest. Check in with me as soon as you hear anything else from Roth."

"Will do. Good night, sir."

"Good night," he said around his own yawn. Fighting the urge to let his eyelids drop, he refocused on the red dots ahead growing ever closer and mentally grasped for a plan to find the girl in Crescent City. He had to find her before catastrophe struck.

He didn't have a recent picture of her, so his only point of reference was her father's description and a list of her favorite activities. Church, work, school and riding bicycles—not much to go on.

She had friends in each activity, but Parker had been adamant that she just hadn't had time for much else. Her master's program really took up almost all of her spare time.

But at least it was a place to start.

Nate spied the large wooden shaft sitting in the middle of the road much too late. When his sedan smashed into it, a hideous scraping vibrated along the underside of his car.

A hundred feet down the road, just as he passed a large white sign with blue letters welcoming him to Crescent City, Colorado, population 26,714, smoke appeared in his rearview mirror. White and airy at first, it quickly began to darken.

"Just great," he mumbled, pulling off the highway and into a little service station. "Nice going, Andersen."

He parked the smoking vehicle—a Bureau-issued, undercover, black sedan—and got out to take a look around. The station was locked up tight with a little sign tucked into the front window. The red arms on the paper clock indicated the shop would open up at seven-thirty the next morning. He glanced at his watch; only a couple hours away.

The lights of the city didn't really begin for about half a mile or so. It wasn't worth it to walk that far looking for a hotel for only two hours of sleep. He'd get more rest in his car.

He reclined the back of the seat, cracked the window, crossed his arms over his chest and fell into peaceful oblivion.

Danielle Keating squinted at the black sedan parked in front of Andy's Auto Shop. She hiked her coverall bottoms up at her waist before slipping one arm into its sleeve. The gray tank top she usually wore underneath was clean, so she wasn't in too much of a hurry to cover it up. Besides, the early morning sun made her simmer when zipped inside the full-body jumpsuit.

With the arm that was still free of the blue sleeve, she shaded her eyes and peered closely into the car's window. Backseat empty. Front seat em—

Whoa!

She jumped back just as the driver's side door flung open, and a dark-haired man with bloodshot eyes stepped out. He rubbed his eyes with the heels of his palms and nodded at her. He ran his tongue over his teeth and yawned but didn't speak.

He squinted in the glare, but she could tell by the slow up-and-down movement of his blue-gray eyes that he was appraising her. It sent shivers up her back, and she quickly shoved her bare arm into its sleeve.

Just because she didn't like being assessed, didn't mean she would back down. Doing her best to maintain eye contact, she leaned a little closer. She waited for him to speak, but he seemed in no hurry. He pushed his large hands into the pockets of his wrinkled khaki pants and jingled keys or loose change there. His broad shoulders stretched the blue cotton of his polo shirt, and he stood somehow both relaxed and erect, leaning against the side of the car.

Finally she could handle the silence no longer. "Having car trouble? Or just needed a place to park?"

He squinted again, this time lifting the corners of his mouth in a half smile, his face suddenly coming alive. "Car trouble. I hit something in the road about a quarter mile back, and then I saw smoke in my rearview...so I pulled over."

"Good thing you did." She nodded, not taking her eyes off of him.

"When does the mechanic get in? I'd like to get it looked at right away so that I can get home."

Danielle's smile faltered for a moment, but she quickly plastered it back into place. Why did men always assume that she was the front-counter help? "She's here now and is happy to take a look. Pop the hood."

The tall man's ears flushed red in appropriate contrition beneath his closely trimmed brown hair, and she took a measure of pride in his shame. He opened his mouth, then seemed to think better of it and hopped back into the car, bending forward to pull the hood release.

Danielle lifted the hood and propped it open, leaning into the shadow. She felt, rather than saw, him move to stand next to her, his body radiating warmth in the already oppressive heat of the unusually mild September. She took a step away, trying to keep her jittery nerves under control. He wasn't necessarily a threat to her. He probably had no idea who she was. Why would he?

Shooting him a sideways glance through narrowed eyes, she sucked in a quick breath before lifting the radiator cap, revealing a normal amount of fluid. The oil dipstick showed normal levels, too.

"Hmm. It's probably your transmission fluid. Let me check."

He shook his head as she shimmied under the car. "But it was running fine."

Sure enough, the pan was leaking copious amounts of dark fluid. "Yeah, you probably hit something that cracked your pan and left your transmission to fend for itself. Hang on."

She scooted out from under the car and turned on her side, peering all the way up at his face. He looked slightly perplexed, but reached out a hand to help her to her feet. She hesitated for a moment before letting him dwarf her hand in his much larger one. His tug gentle yet firm, she immediately found herself on her feet, toe-to-toe and far too close for comfort.

"Thank you," she mumbled, taking a few quick steps backward.

"You're welcome."

Her eyes sought his again, even though she wasn't sure what she was looking for there. His smile was gone, replaced by exhaustion. "Did you sleep in your car, Mr....?" Her voice trailed off, as she chided herself for not asking his name before.

"Andersen. Mr. Andersen."

In her mind she replayed the line from *The Matrix* in a menacing tone and barely managed to keep from laughing out loud.

"Danielle," she said, holding out her hand to shake his. He nodded, looking even more tired than before. "It's going to take me a little while to check out your car more completely and make sure there's nothing else going on with it. Help me push it into the garage, and then you can sit down in the waiting room. We're not usually busy on Tuesday mornings, so you might even be able to get a little sleep."

"Thanks," he said as he leaned into the car again and slipped the automatic into neutral. She couldn't help but notice the messy passenger seat, which seemed inconsistent with the man. While he had tousled hair and more than a five-o'clock shadow growing on his chin, he seemed mostly put together—or would have if he hadn't slept in his car. She'd seen all sorts of cars and their owners since starting at the shop more than a year before. Usually the single guys in ripped T-shirts and stained jeans trashed their cars, not the men with desk jobs and khakis.

"Ready?"

"Huh?" His voice jerked her from her thoughts. "Yeah. Let's go."

Together they pushed the sedan to the garage door, which Danielle quickly unlocked and raised. When the car was settled over the in-floor pit, Mr. Andersen disappeared into the waiting room, and Danielle set to work, glancing every couple of minutes at his slumped form. She wasn't sure what she was expecting him to do, but as long as they were alone together in the garage, she wanted to know where he was.

Nate snorted loudly, effectively ripping himself from the light doze he enjoyed on the hard plastic chair in Andy's Auto Shop waiting room. Leaving his chin resting against his chest, he rubbed the back of his neck with both hands and squeezed his elbows together. The stretch of his arms and shoulders felt wonderful after being cooped up in the car for so long.

He blinked once, his eyes scraping the tender

flesh of his eyelids, and groaned loudly. He rubbed both hands over his face. Two-day-old beard rasped against his palms, and he shook his head slightly and closed his eyes again to let them gain some of the moisture they'd lost during the long night.

He definitely wasn't twenty-five anymore. When he first started with the Bureau, all-nighters and long-term stakeouts were a snap. Even with only stale Funyuns and massive amounts of Yoo-hoo to drink, he'd been alert and thoughtful, great at his job.

At almost thirty-five he had to admit—even just to himself—that he needed to take better care of his body. Especially if his immediate response to a lack of sleep was snoring in a waiting room, even though he should have been on the job. No more all-nighters. It was just that easy. That is, unless his job required it. He'd take better care of himself, but he'd do whatever the job required. Over the last several years as the special agent in charge of the Portland office, Nate did whatever it took to complete the assignment.

He sighed into his hands and blanched at the acrid smell of his own morning breath. He felt his pockets for a stick of gum, but remembered that he'd left the pack in the center console of his car—which he saw through the window was being worked on by the pretty, young mechanic who stood holding a light deep under the hood.

He'd seen plenty of women mechanics in his life but never one quite so cute. That was really the only word to describe her slightly rounded face and innocent brown eyes. Brown hair bobbed around her shoulders and she pushed her bangs out of her eyes as she shifted the light to her other hand and used a wrench to loosen a bolt.

Suddenly she dropped her arms and locked eyes with him. Through the window he felt the intensity of her stare as though she had caught him doing something wrong. He held her gaze for a moment, until she let her eyes fall down and the moment was gone. Not sure exactly what had been lost, Nate decided to put it aside and focus on finding a mint or stick of gum. Eventually he'd have to talk with the woman—she'd said her name was Danielle—and when he did, he didn't want it to be an altogether unpleasant experience for the both of them.

He walked across the small room to the service counter. The chair behind it was empty even though a glance at his watch told him it was nearly eight-thirty. Someone was running late.

Peeking his head over the counter, he spied a small plastic bowl of candy. Just as his fingers wrapped around a plastic-wrapped peppermint, the main door of the office opened with an obnoxious squeak.

"We don't keep any money back there, Mister."

Nate spun around to face a rather short woman flanked by silver crutches that looked to be several inches too tall for her, causing her arms to stick out at odd angles.

Dramatically contrite for being caught red-handed, Nate hung his head slightly and held up both hands, pinching the mint between his thumb and forefinger. "I was just looking for a mint. Morning breath."

"Oh." The middle-aged woman shrugged and hobbled across the slick tile floor, the rubber tips of her crutches slipping with each step. She glanced toward the window where Danielle closed the hood of his car then wiped her hands on a greasy rag as she stepped through the door connecting the garage and the waiting room. "Better pop that in before Danielle gets in here. She hates morning breath."

Nate let out a chuckle, not quite sure if the woman was teasing him or if Danielle really did have a vendetta against bad breath. Figuring his first instinct was definitely right, he quickly unwrapped it and popped the fresh-tasting candy into his mouth in the nick of time.

"Well, Mr. Andersen, it looks like you cracked your transmission pan, but that's all. It'll only cost a couple hundred bucks to replace it, but I don't have a spare part in the garage. I'll have to order it, and it could be a few days. I'm sorry." Danielle's face filled with compassion at the same time he could feel a frown spreading across his face.

He jabbed his hand through his cropped hair. This was definitely not part of the plan, but he didn't have any choice but to take it in stride. Try to be flexible. Admittedly not his strongest trait.

He could call a regional bureau office. They could get him a replacement car within a day. They would also draw completely unnecessary attention to him, possibly jeopardizing his ability to get the job done under the radar.

Pushing the candy into his cheek, he sighed. "Okay. I guess this town isn't that big anyway. I can walk wherever I need to go until it's fixed. Do you have a shuttle that could drop me off at my apartment?"

Nate followed Danielle's glance over his shoulder to the receptionist noisily settling into her chair behind the counter. "Gretchen?" A lilt in her tone changed Danielle's question into pleading.

The other woman held up her hands. "No can do. Jimmy dropped me off this morning. I can't do any driving until my ankle heals. Doctor's orders." She paused for a moment, obviously assessing Nate from head to toe. "But I'll watch the garage until you get back."

"Thanks," Danielle said, in a tone that indicated

she meant anything but. With a nod toward the exit she continued, "Come on, then. I'll take you wherever you need to go."

Nate quickly followed, waving his thanks at Gretchen. "I just need to grab my bag out of my car." He hurried to retrieve the nondescript, black duffel bag from the backseat. Running his fingers over the side pocket, he confirmed that the file with his assignment information was still tucked safely inside, then he walked out through the raised garage door.

Danielle pulled a beat-up truck with the Andy's Auto logo on the door to a stop next to him, and he hopped in. "Thanks for dropping me off."

"No problem. Where is it?"

"The Eagle's Den apartments. Do you know where that is?"

"Sure."

She kept both hands—delicate, fair-skinned hands that looked like they had no business working on cars—on the wheel as she expertly maneuvered through the side streets to arrive at the apartment complex. He had selected them specifically because they offered clean, furnished apartments. Nate calculated how much attention it would draw, and the Eagle's Den had passed his preliminary inspection. The apartment would do nicely—but not too nicely.

After several minutes, the silence seemed a bit

awkward. "So how long have you worked at the garage?" Nate said finally.

"Awhile." Then, as though she thought he was fishing for her credentials, she added, "Long enough to be good at my job."

"So you like it."

She shrugged, keeping her eyes straight ahead. "Sure. Andy and Gretchen are great."

Suddenly she whipped around a corner and they were at the front office of the complex.

"You can drop me here," he said.

"Are you sure?"

Truthfully he didn't know which apartment was his yet. It was his first trip there, so he had no idea where to direct her. "Definitely. No problem." He scooted out of the cab and handed her a slip of paper. "My phone number. So you can call me when the car is done."

"Thanks." She flapped the paper in agreement before accelerating out of the parking lot.

Nate chuckled. She was one strange girl. Evasive with every answer. Obviously a pro under the hood. And adorable as could be.

After checking in at the office and finding his new, temporary home, he sank down onto the dark brown couch in his living room. Flipping open his phone and the assignment folder at the same time, he speed-dialed the number 9, and a familiar voice immediately sounded on the other end of the line.

"Andersen. What's your status?" Mitch Hollingsworth, his supervisor, asked.

"Just got to my apartment. My car broke down just outside of Crescent City, but I'm here now. The car'll be fixed in a couple days."

"What are you going to do until then?"

"I'm going to enroll in the community college. Our guy on the inside said that the Shadow has been snooping around the campus. He's obviously a step ahead right now, and I can't afford not to know what he knows. It's the biggest entity in town, so most of the grapevines will run through there. I'm bound to pick up something that either leads me to the Shadow or Nora." He scrubbed a weary hand across his face. "I'm also going to try to find the church she attends and see what's going on there. I'll check into bike clubs and such. It's not that big of a town so it can't be that hard to find the girl."

Mitch sighed. "Parker James could be the most important witness the state has ever had against Goodwill. His daughter has to be found."

"I know, sir." Nate felt the weight of reality settle once again on his shoulders. He knew the gravity of the situation. They'd already lost one man to a stray bullet in pursuit of Goodwill's conviction in that dark alley a-year-and-a-half before.

Mitch exhaled and said exactly what Nate already knew to be true. "If you don't find the James girl and the Shadow, he'll make sure Parker won't testify against him. Ever."

TWO

The phone in her kitchen rang obnoxiously as Danielle heaved two bags of groceries on the counter. "Hello?" she panted into the receiver.

"Danielle, it's Andy."

She almost returned the smile she always heard from her boss through the phone line, but this time his voice was quiet, sad. Andy McDougal's typically exuberant self didn't produce a smile this morning.

"Is something wrong?"

"Well…" Andy's voice trailed off, tattling that he was going to ask a favor. He never failed to start requests in the same way, but whatever he needed, she'd gladly offer it. "See, my mom's had a fall. Broke her right wrist and sprained her ankle bad."

"Oh, Andy. I'm so sorry to hear that." Danielle had often wondered if Andy was still a bachelor at forty-seven because his mother needed him so often, and he never complained about dropping everything to travel two hundred miles to help her. "I'll be happy to cover the shop for you if you need to go visit her."

"Thanks. I knew I could count on you."

"Anything you need. You know I'm here for you." Andy had been her only family since she moved to Crescent City, and she had only loved one man on earth more.

Blinking furiously at the tears that sprung to her eyes at the sudden reminder of her own failure, she cleared her throat. Her cowardice had cost her her entire world.

She'd failed in the past, but not this time. Swiping at her eyes with the back of her hands one more time, she rubbed against the burning in her eyes. "Is there something else you need me to do while you're out of town?"

Andy sighed softly and started another sentence. "Well…actually there is something else. You know how I've been teaching the Intro to Auto Shop class at the college?"

"Mmm-hmm." Andy left work at four-fifteen every Tuesday and Thursday for the last two weeks to teach at the Crescent City Community College. She knew firsthand that he was a great teacher, but what could it possibly have to do with her?

"While I'm with my mom, there's no one at the college to cover the class, so I was wondering if you might be able to fill in for me. You could close the shop early, and it should only be for a couple a weeks. Just four classes or so."

"Oh." It was the only sound that Danielle could manage in her shocked state. Andy knew her better than anyone. After all, it was Andy who gave her a place to live and a job, teaching her how to be a mechanic when she'd had to start over. He knew just how long it had taken her to open up to him, to get comfortable talking with him.

She hated talking in front of people. Hated being the center of attention. What if someone recognized her? What if someone knew her past? Knew that she'd left her father to die in an alley more than a year before?

Her life was all about blending into the crowd, matching the flowers on the walls. It had to be.

Teaching a class in the largest community in town, wasn't blending. Not by any stretch of her imagination.

She hated letting him down, but she just couldn't risk putting herself on display.

She'd had dreams of the gunman in the alley night after night when she first arrived in Crescent City. It had taken her months to realize that he probably wasn't coming after her. Whatever Goodwill had wanted from her had died with her dad.

But what if she was wrong? What if there was someone out there still looking for her?

"Andy, I'm sorry. I just can't."

"Danielle, I know this isn't easy for you, but I'm begging you. Please. There's no one else even remotely qualified to fill in for me, and there's no one else to look after Mom. I have to go."

Taking a deep, calming breath, she said, "Let me think about it a little while. I'll call you back."

After hanging up, she plopped onto a kitchen chair and stared at the receiver in her hand. What could Andy possibly be thinking asking her to teach a class?

He was her best friend. Her *only* friend. And she really wanted to help him.

But it meant putting a big target on her back.

Hanging her head, so low that her chin rested on her chest and her brown locks fell in front of her face, she rubbed the ends between her fingers thinking about everything she'd done to disguise herself. The short hair, which she'd promptly dyed a deep chestnut color after leaving Portland. The colored contacts to cover her uniquely golden eyes. She'd even dropped about fifteen pounds.

That had been by accident, of course. Too much stress and she couldn't eat.

She was barely recognizable as Nora Marie James—even to herself.

So why am I afraid that someone else will recognize me?

Deep in her heart she heard a voice telling her

that she didn't have to be afraid. She knew that voice, trusted it, but still… "God, if You want me to do this for Andy, You'll have to give me the strength."

As she fell silent, an inexplicable peace filled her heart, and she knew that she could do this for Andy—no matter the cost.

As Nate strolled the ten short blocks from his apartment to downtown Crescent City, brightly colored posters adorned the window of every barber shop and country store. He stopped to read one. Immediately a middle-aged man in an apron walked to the open door of his wood-working business.

Nodding to the vibrant poster, he asked, "You in a band? I hear they're still looking for groups for the battle of the bands at the college."

The other man's eyes traveled up the road, and Nate's gaze immediately followed. "Nope. Just curious about what's going on."

"There's a big bulletin board up at the quad at the college. They post just about everything happening in town there."

"Do you know if they're still accepting students?"

The little man pointed a stubby finger at another flyer, which announced that college registration was still open, and community members were welcome to sign up for two more days.

If he weren't consumed with the task before him, he would have liked to see what some of the other posters offered—theater, concerts and martial arts classes—but he didn't have time for any of that. Crescent City wasn't a vacation destination. Nora James was his sole reason for being here. He had to find her—and the Shadow.

Doubt flickered through his mind for a split second. What if Nora wasn't here? What if this entire mission was a wild-goose chase?

He shook his head and tried to clear away his misgivings. He'd done exactly what he was supposed to. He'd followed the only tip they had. Better to send someone after the girl than let the Shadow have her without a fight.

"Thanks," he said, waving to the man, as he headed farther into town.

As the special agent in charge of the Portland bureau office, Nate didn't get much field time anymore, and he missed it. Most days overflowed with paperwork and bureaucratic meetings. The wind blowing in his face and the sound of his shoes clapping along the cement sidewalk built excitement in his soul as he picked up speed.

Nate shot up a quick prayer of thankfulness that he hadn't had another field agent to send on the assignment. Myles Borden was on his honeymoon.

Heather Sloan was stuck in the office following hip surgery. And Jack Spitz was stuck in a car on stakeout for another case he was working.

He lifted his face to the warm sun. Man, this felt good.

Torn from his thoughts by an annoying ring from his cell phone, he pulled it from the back pocket of his jeans. The display told him that it was coming from Heather's cell phone. "What's up?"

"Have you talked to Mitch yet?"

"We talked yesterday."

She sighed audibly. "Okay. I just remembered that he called the office and wanted me to have you call him. I forgot to tell you." She sounded a little sheepish.

"No problem."

Silence reigned for several long seconds. What was making her so hesitant to speak?

"Heather, what going on?"

She sighed. "It's Jack. He's driving me nuts every time he's in the office. When are you coming back?"

He laughed. Why did adults—moreover, adults with law degrees—insist on acting like kids? "I won't be gone long. I figure I've got two weeks at the most. Longer than that, and I've lost her to the Shadow. And I've lost Parker, too." But failure wasn't an option in this case. "I'll be home in ten days. Twelve, tops."

The college buildings loomed large a couple blocks ahead. The big gray buildings seemed out of place among the quaint shops of downtown, but it was still the hub of the community. He needed to get connected and figure out what the Shadow knew that he didn't.

"Hang in there, Sloan," he offered in his best special-agent-in-charge voice. "I'm almost to the community college, and registration for classes is still open. I might as well see what courses are still open and get plugged in."

"Sure thing."

More than twenty students formed a line leading up to the window in the registrar's office as Nate stepped into the line. Most of them fanned themselves with white and green forms.

"I can't believe this crowd," the teen girl in front of him complained to her friend, an equally young and blonde student.

"Seriously. The add/drop deadline isn't until tomorrow. You'd think more people would wait 'til the last minute."

Starting to get antsy after thirty minutes in line, he finally put his mind on the case and thought through the articles in the case file. It held exactly two pictures of Nora. One was a chubby ten-year-old with long blond hair and brilliant, golden hazel eyes. He bet she didn't look a whole lot like that picture anymore. The other picture was from her driver's license, taken at least ten years before. She had a round face and the same blond hair, just with slightly older features.

But the eyes were the same. He'd never seen that color before—like churning, molten gold with flecks of brown. Stunning.

The team had collected two pictures of her. That was all that were left after a house fire, or so he'd been told. Friends and extended family had been no help. Apparently Nora wasn't a fan of being caught on film.

"Next."

Nate looked in front of him, expecting the next person to step forward, but there was no one there. "Oh," he jumped, hurrying toward the frowning woman behind the counter. "Good morning." He smiled widely, but she refused to return it.

"Add or drop?"

"Excuse me?" Obviously there was a language to college that he didn't remember. He'd lost a lot in the seven years since he was in law school.

The bushy-haired woman rolled her eyes at him. "Do you want to add a class or drop one?"

"Add one. What do you have open?"

She glared hard at him, the wrinkles around her eyes deepening. He smiled apologetically, but it didn't seem to help, her voice gruff as she read from her computer screen, "Auto Mechanics 101. German 200. Math 72, 82 and 120." She rattled off a few other options before saying, "The rest have prerequisites. If you have your transcript, I can approve you for the others. Otherwise, it's too late for you to sign up for them."

He shrugged, uncertain of which class to sign up for. None of these options really suited his academic background. But he reminded himself he wasn't in it for the education. Sure, his J.D.—actually his bachelor's or master's—qualified him for most of the classes offered at CCCC. But he wasn't in it for the education.

The lady on the other side of the desk strummed her fingers on the counter, her lips pursed unhappily.

He needed to make a decision.

Auto Mechanics 101? Danielle's pretty face immediately popped to mind. It wasn't very often he saw a cute mechanic, and there probably wouldn't be anyone like her in the class. But it sounded pretty basic, and it could come in handy considering his recent car trouble. Plus it would be easier to talk to other students in the open forum rather than a typical lecture setting.

"Let's do the auto shop class."

Five minutes and one credit card swipe later, Nate was signed up for his first community college class that night. He just had time to get home, change clothes and grab a bite to eat before heading back for the class.

Danielle rubbed her forearms briskly through her light corduroy jacket. While it had been an unusually warm fall, a stiff breeze this evening brought a cold front and possible snow to the mountains according to the local weatherman. Hurrying toward the building that housed the auto shop, she prayed for courage.

"Lord, please give me Your strength." Then silently she pleaded for safety. Being noticed was the first step to being recognized, and she couldn't go back to her old life. Crescent City meant safety and anonymity, save the select few friends she'd made. But standing in front of a classroom took away that security.

But she'd promised Andy.

She clenched her fist to still the trembling before pushing at the large metal door with the number 102 stenciled above it. It squeaked loudly on its hinges.

Great way to sneak in and hope the students wouldn't notice her right away. She'd been hoping for a couple more minutes to bolster her courage, but every eye in the room turned on her as her work boots clomped on the cement floor and she walked toward the teacher's desk.

With one more silent plea for courage, she turned

around and faced them. In her mind she had imagined them all scowling at her, but as she looked at the thirteen men and three women in the class, she saw mostly smiles and friendly nods.

These were her Crescent City neighbors, built of the same stock as Andy. They shared grocery stores and gas stations, and she had probably worked on their cars. They weren't Goodwill's men, or even from Portland. They didn't know about her past. They didn't know about her dad's murder in the alley.

Just the thought of that night made her chest tighten and her heart speed up, but there was no time to dwell on the past or her part in letting her dad die.

Taking another deep breath and forcing a smile, she greeted them. "Hello. My name is Danielle. I'll be filling in for Andy for a couple of weeks while he's out of town." More friendly nods, but no one spoke. "Andy said that you were discussing spark plugs. Can anyone tell me what you've talked about so far?"

A hand raised in the back row of tables, and she stepped to the side to get a better view of its owner. She pointed to him and opened her mouth to ask his name but stopped when her heart jumped.

"Mr. Andersen? What are you doing here?"

His smile showed off his perfectly straight teeth. "Call me Nate. Just enrolled today. Figured I'd better learn a little something about cars." He chuckled, and Danielle couldn't help the genuine smile that spread across her face at the contagious sound.

He had such a pleasant face, strong yet kind, tanned and handsome. And his eyes sparkled in the fluorescent lights.

Suddenly another student cleared his throat loudly, ripping her from her wayward thoughts. She had no right looking at a man that way. She had nothing to offer him. Nothing but constant fear from a past that always haunted her.

"Nate, I assume that you're not going to answer my question."

He nodded. "That's right. Just wanted to see if I could borrow a book. The bookstore had to order me one."

Another hand raised as well. This from a pretty blond woman sitting in the second row. "Me too. I just added this class yesterday, and the bookstore said it could be a couple of weeks before my book comes in."

"I'm sure we have some books here. Anyone else?" Another young man raised his hand, as Danielle opened the metal cabinet behind the desk. After passing out the books, she opened the spiral-bound grade book that Andy had told her was in the top left desk drawer. "Can you give me your names?"

The woman, probably in her late thirties, spoke up first. "Ivey Platt. With two T's."

The young man announced that his name was Kirk Banner.

"All right. Let's get started." She flipped open her book and asked a twentysomething with brown hair, "What has Andy covered so far with you?"

"The name's Ridley Grant." He smiled and winked at her then prattled on about how much they'd covered in the first few classes.

The rest of the class seemed to pass in a blur. Danielle answered questions and covered the sections that Andy had outlined and left for her. The last thirty minutes were dedicated to hands-on learning, and the group gathered around Danielle as she showed them how to inspect and install new spark plugs. They looked at the old ones and discussed why they were no longer good. Several students—especially Nate—interacted in the discussion, and by the end of the two-hour class, Danielle felt surprisingly calm. Her hands were steady and her voice didn't shake at all.

"Thanks, guys. Have a great night," she said, dismissing them just a couple minutes early. Books slammed closed and stools scraped on the floor as the majority of the students made their way toward the door.

Busy packing up her own bag and locking up

the cabinets, Danielle didn't notice the approach of a couple of her students.

"Danielle?" asked a soft soprano.

She jumped and sucked in a breath so fast that she had to cough several times to clear her throat. "Ivey, you scared me." She finally laughed.

The woman's blue eyes crinkled at the corners and turned softer. "Sorry. I just had a quick question. Kirk can go first." She nodded toward the younger man standing beside her.

Kirk Banner was a handsome, if very rumpled, man probably older than most of his cohorts but trying to look like them. His shaggy blond hair was in complete disarray, and his brown eyes were hard, almost angry. He shrugged boney shoulders that stretched the fabric of his too-tight red T-shirt. "I was just wondering how the grading is going to work."

His tone was nonchalant, but Danielle could hear a flicker of antagonism somewhere below the surface.

"Well, of course Andy will give all the final grades. But I'll be reporting to him on the assignments that are completed and the participation of each student in class."

"Cool." He shrugged again and sauntered away.

Through squinted eyes Danielle watched him leave, hands shoved deep into his pockets, shoulders hunched, and head thrown to the side in a cocky swagger. She couldn't put her finger on any one reason, but he made her uncomfortable. She made a mental note not to be alone with him.

As she turned back to Ivey, she spied one other student in the back of the room still gathering his book. Nate's smile was magnetic, and she found herself not at all afraid of maintaining eye contact with him. His smile reached into his eyes, kind and reassuring. *Good job tonight,* he mouthed.

Her pulse skittered and shivers ran down her arms.

How could one little compliment send her twittering like it did?

He nodded and turned to leave. "Oh, Mr. Andersen. Will you wait a moment please?" He nodded again, but didn't move to join her and Ivey. As Danielle turned back to Ivey, the older woman was rearranging her face into the same friendly smile.

"Danielle, do you think I'm too far behind to catch up in this class?" Ivey's perfect eyebrows pinched together, and her smile disappeared. "I've missed so much, but I just really want to get a better understanding of my car." Her face fell slightly before she managed a quick half smile. "My husband used to take care of all of the car stuff. But he…well, he left me and the kids a couple months back."

Danielle frowned slightly. Ivey was behind the rest of the class, but how could she turn down a woman so obviously hurting. "Well, you are a bit behind. But I could help you get caught up. Andy's shop has been a little slow this week. Why don't you stop by the garage tomorrow afternoon and we can look over the previous material?"

"Oh, thank you! That would be wonderful." She smiled brightly again, grabbed her purse and left the room.

Nate stood by the table in the back of the room, leaning his hip against it, muscular arms crossed over his chest. "Have you ever taught before?"

"Nope. First time."

He picked up his borrowed book. They walked toward the door and down the short hallway toward the parking lot. He opened the door for her to exit in front of him, and she couldn't help returning his grin.

"What did you want to talk about?"

"Oh!" Had she really forgotten that she needed to talk with him about his car? "I found the part for your car this afternoon. They had it at a warehouse just a couple hours away, so it got here faster than I thought. I have a light load at the shop, so I should have it done for you tomorrow morning. Come by any time after noon."

"Thanks. I will."

As they walked past the only car left in the parking lot, the hairs on the back of Danielle's neck stood on end. She hugged herself tightly. She could feel someone's eyes on her. Jerking her head from side to side, she hunted for a body, but couldn't see anyone.

"Are you okay?" Nate asked, concern transforming his face. He gently put his hand on her elbow and warmth seeped up her arm.

"I'm fine. I just… Never mind."

Worry etched lines onto his forehead. "You sure?"

"Yes."

"Let me walk you to your truck, anyway."

"I rode my bike," she admitted.

"Huh?"

With her chin she pointed to the bicycle rack on the far edge of the parking lot. Out of the corner of her eye she scanned the shrubs and shadows for someone watching her. Was it someone from her past? One of the men who had killed her father on another dark night?

Nate let out a full-bodied laugh, tearing her from her innermost fear. "The auto mechanic rides a bike! Ha! That's good."

She shoved his shoulder playfully. "Don't tease me." Betrayed by her face as she tried to keep a frown in place, a smile crept onto her lips. "It helps me stay active, and it's usually so beautiful out."

Nate chuckled again as they moved toward the blue bike chained to the metal rack. She bent to unlock it. Just then a full-bodied shiver ran down her spine, and she jerked around, again trying to find the person watching her. But no one lurked in the shadows, and she couldn't make out any forms in the bushes.

"Are you sure you're okay?" Nate asked again, his frown deeper this time.

She opened her mouth to confess her concern, but remembered that she barely knew the man. Just because he felt comfortable, didn't make him safe. If Andy were home, she could call him to come get her. But if Andy were home, she wouldn't be in the parking lot at the college about to ride her bike all the way home in the dark.

Looking up into Nate's face, she realized that she hadn't answered his question. "Yeah...I'm fine. Just got a shiver for a second."

He nodded and crossed his arms over his chest, assuming she was referring to the wind. "It's getting cold out here. I'll see you tomorrow." He patted her shoulder as she straddled the bike. As she peddled around the bend of the sidewalk, one quick glance over her shoulder confirmed that he was still watching her when she disappeared around the curve.

Biting wind chafed her cheeks as she peddled toward the main road. The sidewalks on the campus were dimly lit, so she picked up her speed, hurrying toward the bright street lights. The ride back to her house really only took fifteen minutes, but it felt like hours, each second spent looking over her shoulder, searching for those prying eyes.

The tangible gaze left her shoulders aching with invisible pin pricks as she sailed past a grocery store and a gas station. She thought about stopping. At least there would be other people around. If someone was really watching her, he was less likely to attack her in the midst of a crowd.

But if he had followed her from the college, then he probably wasn't the type to just leave because she was with other people. More likely he'd just wait her out.

Not a thriving metropolis, most of Crescent City shut down by eighty-thirty. Her digital watch read 8:23, which meant the streets would be deserted in just minutes.

She had to hurry. Hunkering down against the wind, she pumped her legs as fast as they would go. Her hands burned from the cold and her knuckles were starkly white beside the black rubber on the handle bars.

The glowing clock on her microwave read 8:32 as she flew through the front door of her little apartment, slamming it behind her. The deadbolt clicked into place, and she hurried to the window, peering through the blinds into the gravel parking area next to Andy's Auto Shop.

Empty. It was completely deserted.

Her racing heart started slowing down when she sank to the floor beside the little love seat in her living room. As the adrenaline drained from her system, her eyes drooped and her brain shut down.

"Lord, why am I suddenly so afraid?"

THREE

Nate woke with a groan, his neck and shoulders aching from the lumpy couch on which he was sprawled. He rotated his shoulders a couple of times and bent his neck from side to side to make sure that everything was in working order. He tried to focus on the contents of the folder spilled across the coffee table in front of him, but his eyes were blurry, and rubbing them didn't seem to help.

"Coffee," he grumbled, as he pushed himself up toward the mini kitchen. "Must have coffee."

He considered drinking the dregs in the bottom of the pot from the night before but thought better of it. He'd only done it a couple of times before and always as a last resort. Things hadn't gotten that desperate yet.

He rinsed out the pot, scooped frozen grounds into the filter and then pressed the orange start button. The machine was probably older than his little sister Jenny, and she had just graduated from college. But at least the thing worked. Soon the sweet aroma of morning caffeine filled the kitchen and adjoining living room, and he poured himself a big mug. No cream. No sugar. Just the good stuff.

Sighing as he and his mug sank back into the couch, he rubbed his watery eyes one more time. Now he could clearly see the shuffled papers on display. Lots of legal forms, a police report, the accounts of the witnesses and the confessions of two men for their participation in the shooting of Parker James and kidnapping of Nora. Neither had turned over on their leader.

On top of the mess sat the two pictures that seemed to hold the weight of the case.

He took another gulp of coffee and leaned his head back to rest on the couch. Closing his eyes, he thought about where he might find her. Where would she hide out in a small town? Where would she go for comfort in the face of fear?

Parker had said Nora never missed a Sunday service, and if she needed comfort and community, he guessed, she'd go straight to a welcoming congregation.

Hurrying to change his clothes and get presentable, he gulped down the last of his coffee and sprinted to his room. In seven minutes flat he was out the door, ruffling his still-damp hair, so it would dry in the sunlight.

He'd seen a large white building with a steeple

on the hill just a couple blocks from the college. Its central location and large size made it a prime place to start. If she wanted to stay hidden, then finding a large congregation would be important. From experience he knew that small churches usually meant that everyone knew everyone else's business. Bigger church bodies tended to have caring people, but so many of them that one could find anonymity among the masses.

He hiked the blocks uphill with a little hop in his step. Danielle had said to come by for his car in the afternoon, and it was almost noon now. He'd have time to scope out the church, and then walk over to the garage to finally get his car back.

The church building was large and cool inside. He entered the foyer through open double wooden doors leading into the enormous sanctuary. Like so many churches of the day, this one had rid itself of pews. In their place rows of chairs lined the carpets. He guessed there were seats for at least a thousand.

A man with gray hair, wearing a blue T-shirt and black jeans stood at the end of the center aisle. "Help you with something?" he asked.

Nate shook his head. "I don't think so. Just new in town and wondering about the church. When are services?"

"I don't know. I just clean the place." The older

man shrugged then pointed to Nate's left. "The office is thataway."

Nate nodded appreciatively and slowly walked down the short hallway. Sure enough, just a couple of yards down a sign hung above a door announcing the church office. Through the window beside the door, he could see a middle-aged woman sitting behind a large desk, her ear glued to the phone and lips moving rapidly. He entered in stealth mode as she murmured, "You'll just never guess what she said."

When the door clicked closed behind him, the office manager looked up, her smile a little guilty. Then it turned inquisitive as she didn't recognize him. "I've got to go, Ruth. I'll tell you all about it later."

After hanging up the black handset, she said, "Well, hello, there. What can I do for you today?" Her smile was bright, even if her eyes still held questions.

Nate offered her a genuine smile, hoping to loosen her tongue a little bit. "I'm new in town, and I was thinking about coming here on Sunday. What time are the services?"

Without breaking eye contact, she swiped a little brochure from a stack on the counter and flipped it open. "I'm Judith McMurphy—church secretary. So nice to meet you." She held out one hand with her palm facing down. Nate gripped it in an awkward shake.

"Nate," he supplied.

"So, Nate, what brings you to Crescent City?" she asked. A quick glance down revealed that she had moved her hand to cover so much of the brochure that he couldn't read the times listed under her pinky finger.

"I'm a freelance travel journalist. Working on some stories about winter activities in Colorado, so I thought I'd set up shop here for a while and take a college class or two while I'm at it."

Seemingly ignoring his cover ID as a journalist, she said, "Oh, we have lots of you young college kids here at Sunday morning services."

Ha! She thought he was young? That was a laugh. His back still ached from sleeping on that terrible couch, and he could barely go twenty-four hours without sleep anymore, if his drive into town was any indication. At thirty-four, he was far from young—but he wasn't about to correct her.

"What classes are you taking?" Judith asked, leaning a little bit closer to him. He opened his mouth, but she said, "Wait. Let me guess. Journalism?"

He fought the guffaw that bubbled in his chest and instead only let a grin cross his face. "Good guess." If he could pass for the writer type with her, maybe he'd be able to pull off his cover.

The wrinkles around Judith's mouth deepened as she smiled, probably thinking herself the perfect judge of him. "Well, like I said, we have lots of young people from the college here. Let's see…Jud, Shelley and Chris. Oh, and the new guy. He's only been once or twice. What's his name…Kirk."

"Kirk? Kirk Banner?"

"Oh, you know him?" Her eyes popped open.

Nate nodded nonchalantly. He'd briefly met Kirk at the previous night's class. He'd stayed after, talking with Danielle and Ivey. And while there was absolutely no evidence to corroborate his gut feeling, Nate didn't much care for the guy. Something about him just didn't seem right.

"Well, that's wonderful!" Judith's smile widened and she leaned forward so that only a few inches separated them. Tipping her head even farther forward, she said in a conspiratorial whisper, "So, Nate, tell me. Are you seeing anyone right now? I can think of at least three very eligible, lovely girls."

He almost choked on his own tongue, but managed to compose himself quickly. He opened his mouth to speak, not even sure how to respond to that statement, when Judith interrupted him as though she hadn't even asked a question. Ticking them off on her fingers, she said, "Let's see there's Rebecca, she's a freshman. Maybe a little young for you."

Nate bit his tongue to keep from saying, *"You think?"* "Yea, I think someone in her mid-twenties might be a better fit for me. Don't you think?"

She winked at him, as though she knew exactly what he was asking. But he wasn't looking for a date. Just his assignment.

Judith's forehead wrinkled slightly, and she tapped her finger against her pursed lips. "Hmm. There's Danielle. She's quiet, but a very pretty girl. Her brown eyes always look so sad. But you seem the kind of guy who could draw her out." Judith winked and pushed his shoulder.

"Danielle? Huh." Nate's grin didn't even flicker, although his mind immediately conjured her face.

"She's really wonderful! Very sweet. Perhaps a little shy, but I'm sure once you get to know her, you'll find her to be fantastic. Should I look for you on Sunday to introduce the two of you? Oh, what am I saying? Of course I'll introduce you!"

Judith prattled on, a busybody at work, while Nate tried to get his mind off Danielle's soft eyes, rosy cheeks and pink lips. The way the wind had swept her shoulder-length brown hair across her cheek last night in the parking lot had been very becoming. And don't even get him started on her dazzling smile.

He sure didn't mind seeing her as much as he had been lately. Too bad she wasn't his case.

But Judith's plans for his life didn't line up with his own. His plans included a long career with the Bureau, spoiling Jenny's kids—whenever she and her husband decided to grow their family—and hot coffee every morning. One thing his plan did not include was a wife and family of his own.

Thanks to his dad and grandfather, Nate knew he could never make a lifetime commitment.

"Don't worry. I'll introduce you to Danielle on Sunday," Judith continued.

Speaking of Danielle, the clock on the wall on the far side of the office read nearly one-thirty. It was time for him to head over to the garage. His car should be done.

"Thanks again, Judith," he interrupted, grabbing the brochure from where she still had it trapped on the counter under her hands. "I'm sure I'll see you around." With a tip of his imaginary hat, he spun on his heel and started toward Andy's Auto.

"So do you see now how the headlight connects to the wiring and fits into the socket?" Danielle held the old headlight that she'd just changed as Ivey nodded slowly.

"I think I get it. But I just know I'm going to need some more practice. Do you have some time next week?"

Not really. But she felt bad for the other woman. It wasn't her fault her husband had run off. Ivey tried to put on a good front, but her eyes were sad, and maybe a bit guilty. Danielle had seen that same look in her mirror for over a year. "Sure. Let's talk in class next Tuesday and make a plan for a day to meet."

Ivey's smile was appreciative, and she daintily dusted her hands together then held them up in front of her face. "Do you have a restroom or sink?"

"There's one right inside the office on your left." Then she thought better of it. That restroom was never very clean, and it wasn't as though Ivey was a complete stranger. "Actually there's one in my apartment around the side of the garage. The door's locked, but I'll walk you around. It's much cleaner."

Ivey grinned in appreciation and reached toward Danielle's arm as though she was going to pat it, then stopped short and laughed. "I better go wash these."

The pair walked around the side of the building, and Danielle unlocked the door, pushing it open, so Ivey could enter first. Debating whether she should wait with Ivey, she decided that she'd best not leave the front unattended. Gretchen was still at lunch.

As she arrived back at the front of the building, Danielle spied a figure strolling down the road, his hands into his pockets, back and neck straight. She lifted her hand and waved gently, doing her best to tamp down the unruly butterflies bombarding her stomach. Why on earth was she so excited just seeing Nate?

He waved in return, and nodded his head in greeting. She ran a hand over her hair, tucking any stray strands behind her ear. Brushing dust and dirt from her coveralls, she tried not to dwell on the fact that she really was wearing the only thing less attractive than a potato sack.

But there was nothing to be done about it. Anyway, she wasn't trying to impress Nate. He was just a client and a student. No matter what happened, she couldn't drag him into the uncertainty—and possible danger—of her world. She couldn't afford to be attached. If Goodwill ever found her, she'd have to hit the road immediately. No goodbyes, no see-you-laters. Attachments would just make that harder.

Since she wasn't really interested in Nate as more than a client, it would be easy not to let it happen.

Right. She'd just think of him like that.

But her stomach didn't heed her mind, as it nose-dived when Nate reached the large opening of the garage door.

"Hi there," he said, hands still in the pockets of his jeans and shoulder leaning on the doorframe.

"Your car's all done," she hurried to assure him.

"No rush." He looked around. "Where's Gretchen? Did she hide when she saw me coming?"

Danielle chuckled. "Not quite." Gretchen had actually formed a bit of a crush on Nate, and hadn't stopped talking about him since Danielle started working on his car. She would be sad she'd missed his visit. "She's at a late lunch."

"Hmm."

Just then Ivey returned, and Danielle jumped in surprise. She'd forgotten that the other woman was even there.

"Thanks so much, Dan—" Ivey's words broke off as she rounded the building and saw them both standing there. "Oh, hi, Nate. Didn't know you'd be here today."

"Just picking up my car. Cracked transmission pan."

Ivey looked clueless and said to Danielle, "Well, I guess I should get going and let you get back to work. Thanks again for the lesson—I really appreciate it."

"No problem. See you tomorrow at class." Danielle waved at the older woman as she climbed into her black two-door coupe and kicked up dust and rocks as she took off out of the gravel parking area. Nodding toward the door that connected the garage to the office, Danielle indicated that they should go inside. "Your paperwork and keys are at the desk."

Nate followed behind her, his steps steady and even on the tile. After she retrieved his key, and he paid the bill, she walked him back to his car.

"You're all set, Nate."

"Thanks for everything," he said, the corner of his mouth quirked into a grin.

"No problem." She ran suddenly damp palms over the heavy blue fabric covering her hips. Why did this man have the ability to instantly make her palms sweat. With a chill, she realized she'd only felt this kind of reaction once before—on that terrifying night when her father was murdered. Could she be in danger from Nate? Was her body trying to warn her that he wasn't safe?

Or was it just a reaction to his smile and handsome face?

She'd felt uneasy around other men before, and this wasn't the same. He'd never given her a reason to think she wasn't safe with him. But maybe he was a good actor. Maybe her heart was getting too involved, which was bound to end badly. Hadn't she proven that with her father?

It all boiled down to the fact that she knew she could trust him. But how did she know it so completely?

Shoving her wayward thoughts aside when she realized she'd been staring intently at him, she motioned to his car. But he didn't take the hint. "So I've been thinking I should get out and meet more people in town. You know, more than just the people in class. Any suggestions where I should go to get more connected with people our age?" His deep voice was soft, but there was still a commanding presence to him—something in the way he stood, broad shoulders perfectly straight, feet shoulder-width apart. His muscles looked loose, yet as if he could move quickly at a moment's notice.

He took a step toward her, and although there was still a respectable amount of space between them, she shuffled back, falling into the car. "Danielle? You okay?" he asked, grabbing for her elbow to steady her. But the zing shooting up her arm only served to make her knees knock together.

"Yes, fine. Just clumsy, I guess." She tried to laugh it off, but it came out sounding like a choked sob. She searched his blue-gray eyes with her own and saw kindness and concern there. The skin at the corners of his eyes wrinkled, as though he was smiling, but his lips stayed in a straight line.

She'd felt safe here—until *he'd* come into town. Was there a connection between Nate and her sudden fears about her past? Was his presence bringing her nightmares to life?

No. Definitively not.

His eyes weren't cruel. His hand around her arm

offered support not domination. He wasn't a threat. She knew it in her gut.

And she was equally confident that she could handle the danger that she instinctively knew was at hand. She'd be fine on her own.

Gently pulling her arm from his grip, she stepped to the side and took a deep breath. Even if he wasn't a danger to her, she needed her own space.

"Are you sure you're okay?" His face showed concern.

"Yes. I'm fine, thanks. I'll see you in class tomorrow."

He nodded as she walked past him headed toward the next car in need of service.

Danielle's hands shook violently as she sat behind the steering wheel of Andy's work truck the next evening. She'd spent nearly half an hour trying to talk herself into riding her bike to the college again, but memories of the terrifying bike ride home just two nights before still made her queasy.

Squeezing her fingers into a fist, she took control of her quaking nerves. She could handle this. There wasn't anything out there in the fading sunlight that she needed to fear.

That was true, but it didn't remove the clouds covering the sun or the lack of any other people in the vicinity. She was going to have to get out of the truck's cab and walk two hundred yards to the auto shop building regardless of her unease. Taking several deep breaths, she steeled herself for the moment of opening the truck door.

She was stronger than this. And she knew it.

Blowing out a hard breath, she wrapped both hands around the door handle and yanked it open. The telltale click of the door's release rushed through her ears like the air being sucked out of an airplane. Inhaling sharply, she pushed the door open with her foot and grabbed her book bag as she stepped onto the asphalt.

A brisk wind chafed her cheeks as she locked, then closed the door. Immediately moving toward her destination, she didn't see the figure until his hand clasped on her arm.

And she didn't know how loudly she could scream until the sound echoed off the buildings and dissipated into the twilight sky.

FOUR

As Nate rounded the corner into the parking lot on two wheels, he spied a scene that didn't make sense in his mind: Danielle backed up against her truck and a looming figure in front of her.

He'd been running late because he'd checked out three local bike shops to see if anyone working there might know Nora. Now he floored his accelerator to get to Danielle's side as soon as possible.

His headlights illuminated the scene in front of him. A terrified Danielle slid along the side of the garage's truck, obviously trying to get away from the man in front of her. But her efforts were futile because the intruder moved in time with her, never letting her step free.

The headlights of Nate's car washed out her complexion, but he thought she looked paler than she should. When she saw his car, her eyes found his. He doubted that she could see him in the darkness, but he had no problem seeing her and the broad shoulders of the man blocking her escape.

Whipping into a tiny parking spot, he killed the engine, practically leaped from the car as his door nicked his neighbor's vehicle. Keeping his face firm as he strode toward the pair, he didn't let his true concern show. This wasn't like walking into an assignment he understood. His mind really should be on the case, but there was no way he could let Danielle be hurt right in front of him. He rubbed his bicep over his side, reassuring himself with the feel of the butt of his gun in his shoulder holster. Whatever was to come, he was prepared.

The other man turned around, probably at the sound of Nate's clomping boots.

"Nate!" Danielle called breathlessly. She took a quick step around the man and hurried to Nate's side but stopped just before touching him.

He looked at the other man, who pursed his lips and nodded at them. Ridley Grant. All suave moves, perfectly coifed hair and trendy clothes. Nate didn't like him already. "Ridley." He offered only a nod and scowl in return, unwilling to take a step closer and extend his hand for a shake with his classmate.

Danielle took a tiny step closer to Nate, and he could feel the warmth of her body on his arm. He could also see the trembling of her hands as she crossed her arms around her stomach.

"We should get to class," Nate said, looking the other man in the eye and daring him to disagree. Putting his hand behind Danielle's back, he guided her through the rows of parked cars without actually touching her. Ridley stalked ahead of them so that the gap between them quickly became large enough that Nate could put his arm around her shoulders, tugging her gently to his side in a friendly embrace. "You all right?" he whispered.

"Yeah. He just surprised me as I was getting out of the truck."

"Did he try to hurt you?"

"No."

"Are you sure?" he double-checked.

"Mmm-hmm." She nodded emphatically and continued looking straight ahead at the back of Ridley's quickly disappearing head.

He squeezed her shoulder, trying not to think about how well she fit into his side, and she leaned into him even more. "Do you want to tell me what happened? What he said?"

She took a shuddering breath. "He didn't say much really. I'm not really sure what he wanted. I was just getting out of the truck, and then all of a sudden he was there. He scared me at first, put his hand on my arm." She placed her own hand on her forearm to demonstrate. "But when I screamed and jumped back, he just got closer and closer, leaning toward me but not really saying much. Then he touched my hair."

"What do you mean?"

Rubbing several strands of hair between her thumb and forefinger, she cringed at the memory. "I don't know. He just touched it. He ran his fingers through it at the end right here. He just said it looked pretty."

Nate had half a mind to agree with the jerk. Her hair was soft and shiny. Even in the growing darkness, he could see how it reflected the tiniest fraction of light. He didn't blame the guy for wanting to run his fingers through her hair. If he had something more than heartbreak and pain to offer a woman and he didn't have a case to focus on…well, no use wondering about those things.

"Then he leaned toward me, almost like he was going to kiss me."

He went rigid, anger sparking inside him. He knew he wouldn't be kissing Danielle. But a pang in his gut told him he sure didn't want anyone else doing it, either, so long as he was around. "What did you do?"

"I don't know. I guess I just stared at my feet and tried to push past him. But he didn't budge. Then I saw your headlights."

"Are you sure you're all right?"

"Yes. I'm fine." Her body was still shaking slightly, and he hated to let her go. But they were almost to the classroom, and she didn't need Ridley or anyone else thinking that there was something romantic between them.

Dropping his arm from around her shoulders as he used the other to push open the door, he said, "I'll walk you back to your truck after class."

"Thank you." Her voice was soft, and the gentle clasp of her hand on his even softer. She looked up into his eyes and offered him a world of heartfelt gratitude in that one glance.

He certainly understood her fear from Ridley's inappropriate actions. But something else reflected in her eyes. Something had her spooked.

For a second he wished he had the time to hunt it out. But his job wasn't to help pretty mechanics, so he made his way to a seat at the back of the class as Danielle squared her shoulders, shook her head—as if dispelling any worries—and turned to face the class.

"Sorry we're getting started a little late. We'll have to move quickly to get through the material today, so if you have any questions please be sure to ask. Everyone open your books to page 204."

He followed along with the instruction, but frequently had to force his mind back to the classroom at hand. It wasn't as if he needed the college credit, and now that he had time to sit back and look around the room, his brain wanted to think about how any of the people in the room could be related to his case.

Ridley sat straight on his stool, as though it would take a bulldozer to send him sprawling on the floor. Arms resting on the table in front of him, he watched Danielle's movements like a panther watching its prey.

Was he a ladies' man, used to having easy conquests, who'd set his sights on Danielle? Or was he real trouble for her?

Suddenly the guy sitting next to Ridley raised his hand. Kirk Banner. For every clean-pressed line that Ridley sported, Kirk offered a wrinkle and a stain. His low-slung jeans were nearly shredded and his dark yellow shirt showed off what looked to have been a pretty hideous bleach accident. Was he trying too hard to fit in with the younger students?

"Yes, Kirk?" Danielle called from the front of the room.

He ran a hand through his greasy blond hair. "Is this going to be graded?"

Danielle's sigh was silent, but Nate could see her shoulders rise and fall from all the way across the room. "As I mentioned in the last class, I'll be grading you on participation and will be passing along my thoughts to Andy when he gets back. He'll be grading your assignments, the ones you've already turned in and the ones that are coming up."

Kirk sagged a little but didn't look any more attentive than he had before he asked the question.

Just then Nate's pocket vibrated. He surreptitiously pulled out his phone and pressed the button to open the waiting text message from Heather:

Roth says S is in place. Target nearly confirmed.

He and the Shadow were in the same city, and Nate was at least two steps behind. He had to find Nora ASAP.

"All right. Let's head over to the work area, and I'll show you what actual brake pads and shoes look like and where they're located." As stools scraped on the floor and students made their way to the garage side of the room, Danielle turned to the large metal cabinet behind her. Her hands were steady for the first time since the beginning of class. Hunting through Andy's enormous ring of keys, she found the one labeled Cabinet. But just as she moved to press it into the lock, she noticed that the door stood slightly ajar, and the silver lock was covered in scratches. It had been jimmied.

Quickly looking around at her students, she

wondered who would be looking for something in there. It was used only to store auto parts, and a quick glance showed that nothing seemed to be missing. She tried to think of who had been early to class. But the truth was everyone had been earlier than her, except Ridley and Nate.

Kirk yelled from the far side of the old car they were using for teaching. "Is this going to take all night? Some of us have social lives!"

What had his knot wound so tight tonight? She refrained from rolling her eyes at him and instead grabbed the brake pads and shoes for demonstration.

When she rejoined the group, she wedged herself between Ivey and a traditional student with sleek good looks.

Glancing around the semicircle, she spied Nate standing directly across from her. He looked somber and deep in thought when she caught his eye. But then his nostrils flared and eyes crinkled like he was holding back something highly amusing. He just shrugged as if to tell her to continue.

Ivey, who stood to her left, offered a genuine smile and took immediate interest in the discussion of the use for and replacement of pads and shoes.

The rest of the class seemed to speed by, and in no time Kirk—the jerk, as her mind was apt to fill in for her—reminded her about his needy social life. "Hey, it's time to go. Can we get out of here?"

Danielle quickly smiled and nodded. "Class dismissed. I'll see you all at the next class."

Ivey hurried to her side. "Great class! That was so interesting."

"Thanks."

"Are we on for some extra time next week? Maybe on Monday?" Ivey's eyes filled with hope, and Danielle didn't have the heart to refuse.

"Sure. Why don't we meet here at one on Monday afternoon? I was going to come in and do a little prep for class next week anyway."

"Perfect! I'll see you then." Ivey bounced off, her blond hair flying, looking more like a college-aged coed than a mature woman.

The rest of the class had cleared out by the time Nate approached her at the desk. His shoulders looked relaxed, but his forehead was wrinkled, eyes squinting slightly. He looked almost as if he was in pain, so she dropped her bag and reached out to touch his hand, stopping just shy of it.

Touching him could be tantamount to sending an electric current straight up her arm. She wasn't going to pretend that he didn't affect her. Their walk to the building before class, during which he snuggled her under his arm, had been a welcome distraction from her creepy encounter with Ridley. Even now just the memory of it brought a smile to her face, and she wondered what it might be like to have his arm around her all the time.

But it was all useless imagination, so she shifted her mind back to the present, her hand still dangling awkwardly in front of her. Dropping it to her side, she looked into his eyes.

"What's wrong?"

He shrugged. "I've been thinking about Ridley."

"Oh, he's just a pest." She hoped her chin didn't shake at her fib.

"I'm not so sure. I was watching him tonight and he seemed oddly fixated on you. I just want to make sure you're all right." He winked. "I mean, who's going to fix my car if you're not around?"

"Well, the point of this class is that you should be able to fix it on your own."

He laughed. "Not likely. I can't even avoid whole trees in the middle of the road."

She laughed, too, as they moved toward the door. She locked it carefully behind them before walking down the hall.

As they exited the building together for the second class in a row, the hair on the back of her neck stood up again. Tingling sensations ran up and down her arms, and she shivered.

Someone was watching her again. She wasn't imagining it.

At least, she didn't think she was.

Angling her steps toward Nate's warmth, she picked up speed as she moved next to him. He seemed oblivious, as his eyes swept back and forth through the darkness. Did he feel the eyes watching them, too? She was just about to ask him, when they arrived at the truck.

"Well, good night," he said, turning toward his own car.

But fear crashed through her stomach, nearly stealing her breath. What if someone followed her again? Eventually she would have to get out of the truck to get into her home. She just wasn't sure she could do it alone tonight.

And for the first time in well over a year, she wasn't alone. She had someone she could ask for help. But she wasn't very good at doing that, either.

God, if it's safe to let Nate in, please show me. I really need a friend, someone I can rely on right now. If I'm not imagining danger, please keep me safe. Give me Your peace in the face of whatever this is.

Lately it seemed that the more she prayed for peace, the more she felt her life spinning out of control. Subbing for Andy. The spying eyes. The jimmied lock. The butterflies that Nate caused. All of it seemed too overwhelming.

She'd come to Crescent City to run away from

her past, from her father's death. But she hadn't counted on a whole new set of problems.

Nate was nearly to his car, and she had to make a decision.

"Wait!"

He turned, one shoulder lifted in a questioning stance. "You forget something?"

She shook her head and jogged over to him. "This is going to sound really weird, but on Tuesday, I thought someone was following me home. I'm afraid they might try again tonight." His face turned stony. "Would you mind just following me back to the garage to make sure no one else is behind me?"

She'd barely closed her mouth before he agreed. "I'll be right behind you."

The truck practically drove itself back to her home, the headlights of Nate's car bouncing in her rearview mirror. She tried to search for other cars following them, but could see nothing. It wasn't until she arrived at the garage and Nate pulled up beside her that their headlights illuminated her worst fear.

Looking up just to make sure she hadn't been mistaken, she swallowed the bile rising in her throat.

Her front door stood wide open.

FIVE

Nate's grip on the steering wheel turned his knuckles white, and a low growl eased from deep in his throat. That door standing wide open meant that Danielle was in danger. And it was serious.

His stomach plummeted at just the thought.

He couldn't give her as much help as she needed—couldn't afford to have divided attention. But he could help her in this moment. Dropping his chin to his chest, he whispered a quick prayer. "Lord, please protect Danielle and me tonight. I don't know what I'm about to walk into, but I trust that You can protect us."

Feeling the adrenaline rushing through his system, he smacked his open palm against the wheel one more time for good measure, jerked his head back up and shoved his car door open. He stomped around to Danielle's truck, where he could see her stricken face through the window.

"Danielle, keep your door locked. I'm going to go in and check it out. Stay here." He spoke loud enough that she could hear him through the door, but he waited for her to look up and make eye contact before heading in.

"What if there's someone in there?"

He was well protected, but she didn't need to know that. "I'll be fine."

She nodded weakly.

Slipping to the door, he pushed it farther open with his toe, sliding just inside before tugging his Glock from its shoulder holster. Holding it straight in front of him as he entered the room, his feet moved silently on the floor as he approached the first open door on the far side of the room.

"Hello! Is anyone here?" he called into the darkness. He held his breath, drowning out all distractions as he listened for any sound coming from inside.

No response and no sound.

Reaching into the room, he groped along the wall until his fingers connected with a light switch. He blinked as the light exploded to life. He squinted to adjust to the brightness as he swung around, checking every corner of the small room. Following the wall to the next door, he popped it open, plunging his gun into the small coat closet before he realized what it was. His heart pounded in chest, as though it was trying to break free, anticipation rushing through his veins as he swept to the next closed door.

Methodically he moved from room to room until he was sure the entire house was empty. Very little appeared to be disturbed, except for the stacks of papers on the dining room table. They were strewn across the table and floor, wrinkled and torn.

When he was sure it was safe, he hurried back to the truck and knocked softly on the window. Danielle, whose head had been tucked into her chest, bolted upright.

"Come on," he said, nodding toward the light streaming into the parking area from the still-open door. She jerked the truck's door open and stumbled out, falling into his waiting arms. Her entire body trembled, and he could see that her legs wouldn't hold her on their own.

He wrapped his arms around her, holding her tight until he felt her arms snake around his waist. She snuggled under his chin, her baby-soft hair catching on his five-o'clock shadow. She took two shaky breaths into his shoulder, then pulled back just enough to look into his eyes. He'd never seen anyone so vulnerable in his entire life and a rushing desire to protect her almost overwhelmed him.

Too bad it wasn't part of his job.

And too bad any feelings he had were doomed from the start. If the legacy his father and grandfather passed down to him wasn't enough to remind him to steer clear of relationships, his own failure surely was. He'd already broken the heart of a college friend, who he had genuinely cared for. There was no way he would pursue a relationship with someone as sweet as Danielle, when it was bound to end badly.

"Are you all right?"

She blinked and swallowed thickly. "I think so. Is—Is it empty?"

"Did you lock it when you left tonight?"

"Yes."

"Are you sure?" She nodded. "Do you have an attic?" She shook her head. "Then whoever was here is gone." He rubbed his hands over her upper arms and shoulders to warm her and bolster her courage. The sensations running through his body were an unexpected bonus. "Let's go inside."

He kept his hand on her back as she walked through the doorway then carefully guided her toward the bedroom he had checked out. Even the closet was safe. "Why don't you get comfortable? I'll make you something hot to drink." She nodded mutely and wandered off in the direction of her bedroom, while Nate headed to the kitchen.

Opening the white cupboard doors, he hunted for coffee. Instant, whole beans, decaf, regular. It didn't really matter to him. He just needed a hot mug. Coffee had become a friend over the years, a warm source of comfort. He always thought more clearly with a cup of joe in his hands.

And maybe it would keep him from trying to hold Danielle while he should be trying to figure out who was after her—no! Actually he was supposed to be figuring out where Nora was.

But Danielle needed his help tonight. And he could spare a night for a friend. Right?

"Danielle? Where's your coffee?" he called to the other end of the apartment when his search came up empty.

"I don't have any! I never drink the stuff!" she yelled back.

"You've got to be kidding me," he muttered to him-self.

What was wrong with this girl? Well, at least it would help him keep any truant feelings in check. Even if every potential relationship wasn't slated for failure, he'd never end up with someone who didn't drink coffee.

He'd survive until he got home. For now, he'd make do with tea for both of them.

Danielle's arms felt like lead as she opened dresser drawers looking for something more comfortable to wear. Her chest burned, a common sensation. Fear seemed to be doing this to her a lot lately. And she didn't like it at all.

Who had been in her home? Why were they there? Was this related to her past? To Portland?

She'd lived with uncertainty for a long time,

checking around corners, wondering if and when someone would recognize her. Maybe it was unreasonable to think that she'd instantly be able to trust new acquaintances like Nate. But why was she having such a hard time trusting that God would protect her?

She knelt by her bed and rested her elbows on the bedspread. *God, I can handle this. I know I can. But I really hate being afraid the way I've been the past couple of days. If there's really someone following me, please keep me safe.*

When she finally shuffled out of her bedroom wearing a fresh pair of exercise pants and a huge Andy's Auto sweatshirt, Nate was kneeling on the floor, picking up the mess of papers that had been stacked on her table when she left earlier that day. He looked up to meet her eyes, and her insides squirmed.

Offering a wavering smile, she bent to help him.

"Can you tell if anything's missing?" he asked.

Her head swiveled slowly, but nothing else seemed to be out of place. Her small television and DVD player were unmoved. She kept a safe in her bedroom closet with her personal papers and ID, and she'd confirmed that it was intact as well. "I don't think so. What do you think it means if they didn't take anything?"

"I don't know." His blue-gray eyes flashed kindly, and he offered a hesitant smile. "What are these papers?"

"Just receipts from the shop. Notes from Andy to clients. That kind of stuff. It's all for work."

Just then the teapot whistled loudly from the kitchen, and she jumped, nearly landing in his arms for the second time that night. But she would have no more of that. Squaring her shoulders, she stood and turned to the kitchen. "Would you like some tea?"

"Sure." He didn't sound overly enthusiastic, but he stood as well.

He followed closely behind her, and her heart pounded erratically in her chest. The teapot whistle must have surprised her more than she thought.

Danielle pulled two mugs and two teabags out of the cupboard, then poured boiling water over the bag in each one. She dunked the bags several times then threw them away. Handing Nate a cup, she sipped gingerly on hers as she led him back into the living room.

The room felt oppressively silent as neither of them said a word. She tried to read his thoughts through his wrinkled brow and squinted eyes, but he just looked like he was doing a particularly difficult math problem. His eyes seemed lost somewhere in the bottom of his mug, and he was in no hurry to end the silence.

Trying to camouflage her perusal of him, she took another sip and peeked at him over the pink mug. His shoulders were broad, and he stood with unerringly good posture. Strong arms and hands matched sturdy legs and feet. He looked like he belonged in the room—actually like he owned the room.

But she still couldn't tell what he was thinking.

Silence reigned for another few minutes—the only sound the occasional sip and swallow as they drank their tea. It rang in her ears, making her feel alone, even though she could see Nate sitting four feet in front of her.

"What are you thinking?" she finally blurted out.

"Huh?" He looked confused and surprised for a moment, as though he'd forgotten she was there. "Oh. Just wondering if you're going to call the cops."

"Umm… I… Well, I don't think anything was taken. It was probably just some neighborhood kids playing around." The quiver in her voice nearly gave her away, but she swallowed quickly, covering her uncertainty.

His forehead wrinkled. "Still…maybe you should."

She nodded noncommittally. "I suppose you're right…."

The problem was, she couldn't afford to have them come out. What if they asked too many questions? What if they demanded to see her ID? What if they discovered that she wasn't who she said she was?

Too many what-ifs. Too many risks.

He took another large gulp from his mug, finally setting it on the counter. "You don't seem too eager to get the police over here." The corner of his mouth quirked up as if he had a secret.

"Let's just say that the Crescent City Police Department and I aren't on the best of terms."

"Parking tickets?"

She shrugged, letting him think whatever he wanted to.

"That explains the bike." He laughed. She chuckled at that, too. "So, you're calmer now?"

"Thanks. Yeah, I'm good."

"Then I'll get out of your hair. Thanks for the tea." He said the end of the sentence almost as though it was a dirty word.

"Thanks for everything. Thanks for following me home."

His eyes crinkled at the corners and he reached out to squeeze her shoulder before walking toward the front door. "No problem. If you need anything, just let me know."

"Okay."

With that he turned and closed the locked door behind him.

"Hi, Heather," Nate said the next morning, after looking at the screen on his cell phone and answering the call. "How's everything at the office?"

"Good."

"Anything to report?"

"Not really, sir. Myles and Kenzie just got back from their honeymoon. Myles will be in tomorrow, and Kenzie called to say they had made it back from their cruise and were settling into the new house."

Heather continued talking about the sometimes sickeningly sweet lovebirds, while his mind wondered to the night before, to Danielle's face when she first saw her apartment door standing wide open.

She'd tried so hard to look like she had it all together, but he had a gut feeling she was faking at least part of her bravado. She'd collapsed into him, her body shaking from head to toe. And, truth be told, he'd been shaken up by the turn of events as well.

So even though he knew he needed to check out a couple more bike shops and a few other churches in town, he'd sat in his parked car outside her apartment until the sun came up that morning to make sure that she didn't get any more uninvited guests. All had been peaceful, but something about Danielle's situation still didn't sit right with him. Even so, he just couldn't focus on her small-town concerns—even if he wanted to. He had bigger fish to fry.

"Nate?" Heather's voice sounded concerned.

"Hmm?" He'd missed whatever she was asking him.

"I said, 'Did you need something?'"

He'd called and left her a voicemail as he was leaving Danielle's. He'd thought it couldn't hurt to check out a couple of the guys in his class that were hassling Danielle. "Yes, I need you to run background checks on these two names. Ridley Grant and Kirk Banner."

"You think one of these guys might be the Shadow?"

"Probably not—they seem too amateur. But they've been hassling someone I keep running into."

"Mmm-hmm. 'Someone you keep running into?' Tell me about her. Where'd you meet?"

Heather's insinuation was obvious by her tone and, for some reason he couldn't name, it got under his skin more than her usual teasing. "Do I need to remind you that you're speaking to your supervisor?"

Her laugh twinkled lightly over the phone. "I

have every respect for your position as the Special Agent in Charge. But may I remind you that we've been friends for nearly ten years. I know you better than you think."

Clearing his throat, Nate barked, "Then you ought to know that I'm not looking for anything other than Ms. James and the man who's after her in Crescent City. Long-term relationships in my family don't work, and I have no interest in getting mixed up in anything that's doomed from the start." His voice turned razor-sharp. "So do me a favor and quit acting like I'm not paying attention to my assignment. And run those names for me."

"Sure thing, Boss." Heather's voice was still laced with laughter, and he grumbled to himself as he slammed the phone shut.

Where on earth would Heather get such a crazy idea about him and Danielle? She didn't even know Danielle's name. Their relationship was strictly coincidental. Even after he wrapped up this case, there wouldn't be anything between them, no matter how cute and funny the mechanic was.

He sat down hard on the couch in his apartment and leaned his head back against the itchy fabric. He took several long, calming breaths as he ran his fingers through his unusually shaggy hair. But he couldn't contain his emotions for long. Moments later, his blood started to bubble, and he jumped to his feet, pacing the small living room.

Why was he suddenly so agitated? Why did he feel like he was breaking a promise?

He grabbed for his cup of coffee, tilting it back, then spitting it back out. The cold java tasted terrible. It had been cold this morning when he got home, but he'd sucked down an entire mug of the sludge just for the caffeine. He'd had enough then, and there was no need to drink more cold coffee.

The problem was that he was running on no sleep, and his body was screaming at him.

Finally he threw himself onto the couch, his feet hanging over the armrest. He crossed his arms over his chest and closed his eyes, hoping for a shred of sleep. But his mind was still running, jumping back to Heather's teasing and Danielle's face.

Heather had teased him plenty before about women, and it never bothered him the way it did now. So what was different this time?

He tried not to dwell on thoughts of long-term relationships—or even short-term ones. It wasn't something he was interested in. The legacy that ran through his veins was something he'd much rather forget, and something he had no desire to continue.

Nearly sixty-five years before, Jed Andersen had left his wife—Nate's grandmother—for his young mistress. Ten years later, he left his second wife for an even younger woman. Three wives and a disastrous example of fidelity for his son was all Jed left to his family when he died a few years ago.

As a child, Nate had revered his dad and thought that he and his mom were happy, living out a fairy-tale life. As a teenager, he knew better. His mother's sadness permeated every corner of their life in that run-down house in a rough neighborhood of Portland. He'd watched and done nothing as his father's affairs destroyed their home.

When he came to know the Lord early in college, Nate had promised himself that he'd never hurt a woman like that. Then he'd met Amber and Georgia at a party their junior year of college. He'd spent a lot of time with the amazing girls, quickly becoming good friends with them both. But Amber was special—everything he'd ever hoped to find in a future wife. He was sure he could make her happy.

Until he made his intentions clear.

"What about Georgia?" Amber had said. "Aren't you in love with her?"

He'd been so shocked that the willowy girl could have pushed him over with her pinky. "But I'm crazy about you, Amber."

The sob behind him made him jump, and there stood Georgia. Her bottom lip quivered, but all he could see was the pain of her heartbreak reflected in deep green eyes. She'd thought he loved her.

How could he have led her on so unintentionally?

Because of his mistake, Amber had refused to speak to him. Not only had he hurt Georgia, but he'd also lost his chance with the woman he really wanted.

Adrift without a rudder, Nate had sought advice from anyone who would offer two cents until his dad had clapped him on the shoulder. "Welcome to the family, son. This is what we Andersens do. With a little practice, you'll get better at keeping the girls from finding out too much."

Nate hadn't been trying to keep anything from anyone, but he'd still managed to wound a girl he genuinely liked. It's what Andersens did.

But not if he stayed far enough away from all of them. Since he couldn't control the legacy, it would end with him.

His mind refusing to relax, still running through the story that had led him to that choice, Nate hopped off the couch, grabbed his jacket and marched toward the door, refusing to think about why that choice was suddenly bothering him. A long walk might help clear his head of painful memories and unwanted feelings for his mechanic.

But what he really needed to do was solve the

case. Get Nora and the Shadow taken care of. And get back to Portland.

That would put these pesky feelings right where they should be—two thousand miles away.

SIX

Danielle woke with stiff muscles and pounding temples. Her jaw felt like she'd chewed rubber all night long, and piercing pain shot through her neck when she twisted it slightly. She tried to relax, but her muscles had been knotted tightly all through the night, and now she was paying the price.

This was her own fault.

Why hadn't she been able to protect her dad? Why had she had to run away? She had really liked her life in Portland.

Mostly she really missed her dad. But he wasn't back in Portland, anyway. Every now and then fond memories of her friends from the grad school program would sneak in. Her mind would wonder to what her classmates were doing these days. They'd have graduated and be working at architecture firms, designing buildings across the country.

Exactly what she should be doing. Maybe she'd be working on a new hospital building or designing a skyscraper. Or she could be working for individuals, creating homes that her clients would love. Her options had been wide open.

But when her father died, her choices had been drastically reduced.

Although her life had taken a different path, she actually liked working at Andy's Auto…and she was happy here in Crescent City. Until something from her past started following her. It had to be from her old life. Nothing else could bring her so much fear.

The memory of her front door standing open sent a terrifying tremor down her spine again. Someone had been in her home. What if it had been someone like Ridley Grant?

Another shudder twitched through her at the mere thought. She didn't like where her mind was taking her. It was time to get out of bed and think about something else.

Still lying down, she shook her limbs gently and stretched to work out the kinks from the stressful night of sleep. Chancing a glance at the digital alarm clock to see if she had overslept, she carefully massaged her stiff neck.

A smile broke across her face when she realized that it was only seven-fifteen. The shop didn't open until ten on Fridays, so she rolled over and pulled her thick quilt up to her chin. Closing her eyes, she waited for sleep to reclaim her.

But fifteen minutes later the pain in her shoulders

still kept her awake. Maybe a swim in the heated pool at the YMCA would make her feel better. Or a soak in the hot tub. Just the thought of being weightless in the warm water made her grin.

She gingerly rolled out of bed, got dressed and picked up her gym bag as she headed out the door. She swung through the kitchen and grabbed a banana for breakfast, picking up her keys and eyeing the haphazard stack of papers on her table. The ones that had been on the floor the night before. She took a deep breath and strode straight for the front door, mentally putting the incident behind her. All she could do was her best to stay safe.

The kitchen chair was still wedged under the front door handle, so she moved it aside and stepped into the early sun. The morning was cooler than she had expected, and she pulled her jacket tighter around her. She double-checked that the door was locked, then pocketed her keys.

As she approached Andy's truck, it was leaning to the left. Sure enough the passenger's side front tire was flat. She huffed and put her hands on her hips.

"God, why is it always one thing after another?" she asked aloud. She could fix the tire, but it would take too much time. She didn't particularly want to start her day off fixing a tire, either.

She checked to see if she could tell why it had

gone flat. She didn't see any obvious nails or holes. She could just fill it up, but what if it went flat while she was at the gym? Then she'd have to put the spare on and she would still be late getting the shop open.

Hands still on her hips, she spun around and spied her bicycle locked to the side of the garage. Well, it would have to do.

Her stomach took a nosedive, and it made her pause for a moment. Was this really a good idea? What if someone had let the air out of her tire, trying to force her to use the bike? Or what if that person was watching her even now, waiting for her to be out in the open so he could make his move?

Her head snapped side to side, but she didn't see anyone around.

Taking a couple deep breaths, she forced herself to relax. *Dear Lord, please help me to calm down. This is getting a little bit ridiculous. I'm sure there's probably nothing to worry about this morning, but...well...please just keep me safe. Amen.*

As she peddled the couple miles into town, the morning sun peeked over the horizon, bathing the town in light. All-in-all the ride to the gym was much nicer than she'd expected. The brisk wind hitting her cheeks made her feel awake and alive. Her legs loosened up after such a tense night of sleep, and her nerves calmed down as she steered her way through residential neighborhoods where moms walked their kids to bus stops and dads took trash cans to the curbs. Having other people around reassured her.

By the time Danielle arrived at the YMCA, her reason for needing a swim had changed from sore muscles to the chill of the air. Hurrying into the lobby she whipped out her membership card to show the attendant then hustled toward the locker room.

Teeth chattering she kept her eyes on the floor, her mind only on the thought of the heated pool.

Suddenly she slammed into someone. Already off balance by the large gym bag on her back, she toppled quickly to the floor.

"Oh, man. I didn't see you, Danielle."

She looked up to see who she'd collided with and was met by the laughing eyes of Ridley Grant. He held out his hand to help her up.

She wasn't quite sure she wanted to touch him, even for a boost from the floor. He gave her the willies. Surreptitiously glancing around, she checked to see if there were other people nearby. The last time they'd been alone together, he'd cornered her in the parking lot.

She chanced one more quick look to see if perhaps Nate was coming to rescue her again, her hopes lifting.

Of course he wasn't there. She was being absurd.

But there were plenty of other people headed toward the locker rooms, so she gripped his hand and allowed herself to be tugged to her feet.

"You okay?" Ridley stepped even closer to her, and she took a mirrored step back.

"Fine, thanks."

"You sure? If you're hurt, you shouldn't work out. You could skip your swim, and I'll take you to breakfast."

His last words put her senses on immediate alert.

Taking another careful step back, she asked, "How did you know I was going for a swim?"

His face looked shocked for a second and then quickly fell back to neutral. His pale eyes registered a strange emotion for just an instant. "I—I just thought you might like to swim. You were headed toward the pool."

Just then she heard her name being called. "Danielle! Danielle!" Ivey jogged toward them, waving cheerfully. "I didn't know you worked out here," she continued, obviously missing the strain between Danielle and Ridley.

Danielle tried to smile, but was sure it came off as more of a grimace. "Hi, Ivey. How are you?"

"I'm great. Are you just getting here? Do you want to head to the locker room?"

"Yes!" She pounced on the chance to get away from Ridley and practically dragged Ivey down the hall by her arm.

"I just thought class was so good last night," Ivey prattled. "I can't believe how much I'm learning. It's been so fun! I feel like I should send Jack a thank-you note for leaving."

Danielle tuned out the chatty woman, quite certain that she had to have been a cheerleader at some point in her life, and tried to focus on what was going on. Why did she feel like Ridley was stalking her? Could he possibly be tied to her past?

"Danielle? Danielle?"

"Oh, what?

"Did you hear me?" Ivey looked confused and waved her hand in front of Danielle's face. "I asked if I could come in early to class on Tuesday. I think I need some more help."

"Oh, sure. No problem." Tucking her bag into a locker, Danielle asked, "So how long have you been a member here?"

Ivey smiled. "Oh, it seems like forever. I can't believe I've never seen you here before."

Danielle laughed. "Oh, we probably did see each other before. We just didn't know each other."

"You're probably right. Well, I'm off to the elliptical. Maybe I'll see you later." With that Ivey strode out of the locker room.

Danielle let herself envy Ivey's carefree nature for just a moment. Even after her husband's abandonment, the woman remained cheerful. From all their interactions, Danielle had a gut instinct that Ivey knew how to find the good in every situation and was able to move past the hard things in life.

But there was no use wasting time on wishful thinking, so she squared her shoulders and turned toward the pool entrance.

The water of the indoor pool was crystal clear as Danielle dove into the deeper end. The bubbles leaving her nose as she exhaled tickled her face, until her head surfaced and she pulled her arm in an arch over the water and cupped the water again, propelling her forward. She kicked her feet in short bursts, until she was just feet from the wall. Tucking into a quick flip, she shot her feet toward the wall, pushing off with all the power she could muster.

Every ache and pain that had kept her from going back to sleep that morning disappeared as she sliced through the empty lap lane. She felt light and free, and almost as bouncy as Ivey had looked. She turned her head and sucked in a breath, taking the time to smile.

Thank You, Father, for this beautiful morning. For the sunshine and this warm water and the way that I feel safe here, now.

Another swimmer jumped into her lane at the

opposite side of the pool, and she had to stamp down her urge to ask him to find another one. There were plenty of other lanes available. Why was someone bothering her peaceful swim?

As the two swimmers passed in the middle of the pool, Danielle drew a breath and almost swallowed a lung full of chlorine water. She recognized the shaggy hair of Kirk from class. He was the third person from her class that she'd seen just that morning. Did everyone go to the same gym?

What a strange coincidence.

Despite the warm water and physical activity, Danielle's body suddenly began shaking, and she couldn't break the feeling that it *wasn't* just a coincidence that Kirk had chosen her swim lane. She swam to the edge of the pool and hoisted herself onto the ledge, grabbing her towel and wrapping it around herself.

Heeding the warning signs about running, she walked quickly toward the locker room, only to be stopped by Kirk's echoing call, "Yo, teacher!" His voice bounced off the ceiling but didn't seem to disturb the three other morning swimmers.

She turned slowly to face Kirk's curled lip and squinted eyes, as he jumped out of the pool behind her. Inwardly quaking, she put on a brave face. "Well, hello, Kirk. Good to see you. Did you have a nice swim?"

"Yeah, whatever. Listen, are we going to have an

assignment this week? I might have to miss some classes."

Her brows furrowed, and he just glared at her. Why did he always look so angry? "I'm sorry that you need to miss some class. If you have an emergency, we can reschedule your time in the shop."

His scowl deepened. "I'm going to Vegas with my bros."

She almost laughed out loud. "Then you'll need to get notes from someone else in the class and make up the assignments listed on the syllabus."

Kirk shrugged. "That's not very fair." There was no stopping the snort that escaped through Danielle's nose, and hiding the snicker behind her hand didn't work, either. "I'm serious, man," he said. "It's hard to get used to a new class and everything, seeing as how I started late and all."

She gave him a pitying smile. The kid really was clueless. "Okay, fine. If you want to get the notes in advance, come in early to class on Tuesday and we'll look at the next assignments."

He shook his head. "Oh, I can't make class on Tuesday."

"Thursday then?"

"Whatever."

"So you'll be there on Thursday?" Her voice rose more than she was hoping it would, but the guy was infuriating.

"I just said I would."

No, he hadn't! Instead of yelling at him, she spun and marched toward the door to the locker room. Her peaceful, relaxing swim had been ruined by a knucklehead.

She skipped the shower, suddenly longing for a hot cup of tea in her own home. Bag in hand, she headed out to her bike, hoping this ride would be as relaxing as the one to the pool.

Who would have thought that she'd need another relaxer after her workout?

The wind in her hair, the sun shining on her face as her bike sped down the road, she managed another genuine smile. She liked this feeling almost as much as slicing through the water.

Just then her front tire hit a small pothole, and it didn't recover like it should have. The handlebars felt loose, nearly disconnected from the front tire. She squeezed her brake, but nothing happened. She squeezed harder.

Still nothing.

She glanced down toward her rear tire, where the brake wires should have been connected. The black rubber tubing waved wildly next to her foot.

Her head shot up and she looked straight forward trying to figure out what to do.

The road had a slow but steady decline, so she continued picking up speed even though she'd stopped pedaling.

Her heart pounded in her chest as her eyes darted for a side street she could pull onto. But there was none. Only a ditch and wooded area on her right. A median blocked any hope of crossing to the other side of the road. At the speed she was going she would certainly be injured if she tried to pull into the uneven grassy area.

The road took a sudden dip, and she clung to the wobbly handles as she picked up more speed. She was going to fall, and it was going to hurt. A lot.

Frantically she tried to look behind her to signal a passing car for help.

And then she saw it. A large navy blue SUV pulling up behind her.

At first she thought the driver saw that she was in distress. But then it pulled so close that she could feel the engine's heat on her back through her jacket. It was tailing her. Someone had sabotaged her bike. And now they were going to finish the job!

She pumped the pedals faster, trying to pull away from vehicle, but knowing that she was no match for the big engine. It was useless. She just didn't have a choice. She had to get through this.

"God, please don't let this be the end. Let me make it through this. Please." The words sounded ragged between her gulping breaths.

Of course she hadn't told anyone where she was

going. Why hadn't she called Nate and asked him to take her to the gym instead of riding her bike? He'd said to call if she needed anything.

The SUV backed off for a moment, and she let out the breath that seemed to choke her. Then the engine revved loudly as it pulled even with her and sidled up next to the bike. It was a Ford Explorer with tinted windows, so she couldn't see the driver, who had maneuvered the car to within an arm's length of Danielle.

She let out a little yelp as it slid an inch closer. Maybe she needed help, but there was no one!

God, protect me, she silently prayed just before cranking the handlebar toward the ditch.

SEVEN

Every bit of Danielle's body screamed in pain.

She tried to gather enough force in her lungs to actually scream out loud, but she couldn't seem to catch her breath. She choked and coughed until she managed a slight wheeze, but still the tightness in her chest was almost unbearable.

Gathering her bearings, she tried to push herself up, but the cold ground beneath her was a trap from which she couldn't escape. Blades of crisp grass poked her back through her sweatshirt, and dirt and chlorine assaulted her nose. Her skin itched as she tried to push herself up again.

The blue Explorer would be on her if she didn't get up. She had to hurry.

Despite her body's reluctance to move at her prodding, she managed to roll over and arch her back enough that she could see the edge of the pavement above. She couldn't see anything else, but she heard car tires send gravel on the shoulder flying. Maybe someone had seen the accident and was braking to stop and help her.

She let her head rest back on the ground, ignoring the dead grass she was sure was already sticking out of her ponytail, waiting patiently for someone's help.

But several seconds ticked by, and the car that she expected to see still wasn't visible from this angle. Managing a deeper tilt of her head, she tried to see what was going on on the road, but the movement produced nothing interesting and only caused her back to spasm wildly.

What if no one saw her? What if she was out in the cold all day and night?

Angling her arm to her back, she groaned as she reached for her gym bag, only to realize it wasn't still hanging around her shoulders. The bag and its contents were strewn across the ditch several feet away. Her wet towel and red one-piece suit lay like odd clumps of wild flowers. Then the sun glinted off of what she assumed were the pieces of her dismembered cell phone.

Could this get any worse?

Of course she could take care of herself, but at some point—like this precise moment—it would be nice to be able to call a friend. Or at least Nate.

And then she heard the sound of gravel crunching. Another car? She looked up far enough to see a pair of tennis shoes and jean-clad legs standing beside the blue Explorer.

Blood pounded through her veins and thunder roared in her ears. Dark spots danced before her eyes as she tried to push herself up, and she knew she was toast. Whoever was standing on the side of the road right now had tried to kill her, and he was coming back to make sure he got the job done right this time. And here she was, helpless.

"God, please let me get through this," she whispered desperately.

Like a tidal wave, adrenaline swept through her body, and Danielle jumped to her feet, pain not even registering. Her heart pumped and her limbs moved of their own accord.

She didn't take the time to get a good look at her pursuer. Instead she spun and sprinted into the woods behind her. It wasn't until she was more than fifty yards into the trees that she ventured a glance over her shoulder to see if she was still being followed.

A thin man in a black jacket, red baseball cap pulled low over his features and jeans entered the woods and ran after her at full force.

Danielle urged her limbs to keep moving, but the initial energy burst began to fade, and her muscles felt weak. Roots jumped out of the ground, and she stumbled over them.

Her mind searched for an answer, a place to

hide. Where could she go? The garage was much too far away. Anyway, her key was back in her gym bag or somewhere in the middle of the ditch. Andy didn't live too far, but he was out of town. Of course! This was just her life.

Was there even a safe place for her to hide?

She dodged a large branch jutting out in her path only to catch her toe on a large root, which sent her flying to the ground. Piles of red and yellow leaves barely cushioned her fall and she let out a loud grunt.

The palms of her hands stung and her knee felt bruised, her ankle tender. For a split second she considered staying put, just lying on the ground, waiting for her pursuer to find her. Then this would all be over.

She wouldn't have to live in fear anymore.

She wouldn't be living at all.

That thought jerked her back up to her feet, renewing her energy. With a swift glance at the figure gaining ground behind her, she shot forward.

"Lord, I don't want to die yet. Please don't let me die."

The memory of her father's body sprawled in the alley the last night he'd been alive flashed in her mind's eye. Goodwill had already taken the best member of their family. There was no way she was letting him take the rest of it.

Veering left, then right, she deftly avoided tree limbs and fallen branches. She jumped over a stump just as the sun broke free of the cloud that had hidden it. Light reflected off of something red about two hundred yards in front of her.

The red fleck flashed again, then disappeared, followed by the glitter of a metallic green paint job.

A car.

The street!

She was almost through the woods. As her legs pumped even faster, she began to make out the black asphalt.

And another grove of trees on the far side of the road.

Her heart plummeted.

There were no buildings in which she could find refuge. No random offices where secretaries sat behind their desks ready to call 911 at her first scream.

She could hear twigs breaking behind her. Strangely she had expected her follower to sound like a bull tearing through the trees, but he didn't. But there wasn't time to think such random things.

Just as she broke through the tree line, the image of Nate's face came to mind. She dismissed it as another reminder that she should have called that morning to ask for a ride. Frantically she looked up and down the now deserted lanes. Which way to go?

Nate came to mind again, and this time it clicked.

He lived just a few blocks away.

She took off at a sprint in the direction of Nate's apartment complex. *Please let him be home,* she prayed silently, her chest too tight and breathing too shallow to manage any spoken words.

When her side hurt so badly that she wasn't sure she could keep going, she chanced another peek over her shoulder. Red baseball cap was still on her tail. Looking straight ahead, she saw her only hope right before her.

Nate's apartment building stood three stories directly in front of her. She hurdled a low fence and raced up the steps to the top floor. She glanced frantically at the numbers below the door knockers. Nate had put the address on his paperwork when he picked up his car. But she couldn't remember it. Was it 1131? 1132? 1133?

Definitely 1133.

If she had been a bigger build, she might have knocked the door clean off its hinges as she crashed into it, but as it was, she just made a loud thud and gave herself a sore shoulder.

Pounding on the door with her fists, she yelled, "Nate! Nate! It's Danielle!"

She couldn't hear anything through the door, so

she yelled louder, adding the thump of her foot to the ruckus.

Over the landing's half wall, she could see the man in the black sweatshirt jump the same fence she had just moments before. She would be toast in short order if Nate didn't answer in time.

EIGHT

Nate had just spit out his toothpaste and turned off the bathroom faucet when he heard a commotion outside. Muted thumps and wild yelling sounded near his front door. Grabbing a blue T-shirt to match the jeans he was already wearing, he pulled it over his still-damp hair as he ran toward his foyer.

The noise got louder, and he thought he recognized his name among the shouts coming from the other side of his door, but the banging definitely wasn't on his door. Flinging it open, he stared at the back of a wildly flailing young woman. Her short brown hair was pulled back and covered with dead grass.

"Nathan Andersen!" she sobbed into the door across the hallway. "Where are you?"

"I'm right here." He kept his voice composed, but she still jumped when he spoke.

Danielle spun, eyes wild and rimmed in red. She fell against him, pushing them both into his apartment. Her shoulders shook with what appeared to be both sobs and ragged breathing.

"Calm down, Danielle." He rubbed a large oval on her back, whispering soothing words into the top of her head and holding on to her arm firmly with his free hand. She leaned on him as though she had no strength of her own, but her body still managed to produce ragged sobs.

She looked up into his face, fear and anxiety clearly etched on her pretty features.

And then suddenly her hands and arms were flailing everywhere, and words poured from her mouth in a deluge. "He was right behind—I didn't see him. He ran me off—my bike. I was running— I didn't have anywhere else to go. I thought you weren't here." Tears instantly filled her eyes and began running down her cheeks, the silver tracks like raindrops on a window. "I didn't know where else to go."

"It's okay. I'm glad you came here." He couldn't afford to be distracted from the case, but he couldn't ignore someone in need, either. Especially since she was already growing on him.

He cupped both of her hands between his and looked right into her watery brown eyes, noticing that one was severely bloodshot, as she blinked it rapidly. "Slow down. Tell me what happened."

She took a deep gulp and when she finally spoke, her voice was thin. "I went to the gym.

My truck had a flat tire, so I took my bi-ike." Her voice broke, but she swallowed, dipped her head and continued. "I was riding back to the garage, and a blue Explorer ran me off the road. Then someone chased me through the woods. He was right outside."

Nate's gut clenched. Why would someone be after Danielle? This plus the break-in? Was she mixed up in something and in over her head?

Biting the inside of his cheek, he pushed all the questions he wanted to ask to the side. He still had time to find the man who had chased her here. He might still be outside.

"What was he wearing?" She stared at him blankly. "The man who chased you. What was he wearing?"

She sniffed, reaching up to cover her left eye with her hand, wincing at the pain there. "A black sweatshirt and jeans. And a red baseball cap."

Nate spun to grab his gun from its holster from where it lay on the coffee table. With a practiced thumb, he flipped the safety off and ran toward the door. Her brows kneaded together, as though she was trying to understand what he was doing with a gun. "Stay here."

"No!" she cried. Every one of her pretenses was gone as she clung to his forearm.

He frowned, fighting his own urge to stay and comfort her. But if the guy was right outside his door, he could end this entire thing for Danielle right now. He couldn't pass up this chance. "Sit tight—I'll be right back. Lock the door behind me and don't open it for anyone but me."

She followed him to the door, one eye huge, reflecting the light from the ceiling fixture, the other closed tightly and seeping tears. She looked so young and vulnerable, and he didn't even think to put a stop to his impulse.

He just leaned in and kissed her.

It was quick and chaste, and it sent his pulse pounding more than the knowledge that he might have to pull the gun tucked into his waistband in a few seconds.

Danielle just blinked and nodded as he turned and raced out the door. He couldn't wipe away the image of her stricken face as he rounded the corner of his building and changed his pace to look like any ordinary resident out to get his mail.

Eyes darting into every corner, through every shrub, he meticulously scanned the apartment grounds. It wasn't an enormous complex, so he made quick work of the walk around. He only ran into two people: the maintenance man and a young woman jogging along the paved circumference of the buildings.

No sign of even a leaf out of place. The guy was gone.

Nate traipsed back up the steps to his building,

shoulders sagging. Had he missed his chance to find Danielle's pursuer? What if he never showed himself again? Would they ever find out who was after her?

When he finally arrived back at his apartment, he immediately tried to open the door. The handle didn't turn, and he jiggled it a little more to make sure it wasn't just stuck.

Then he heard a small shriek come from inside the apartment.

"Danielle, open up. It's just me. I'm sorry I scared you."

Several seconds ticked by. The light behind the peephole disappeared as though she were looking through it to confirm it was him, then he heard the deadbolt click and the handle shook. The door opened a crack, and Danielle peeked out.

He cracked a half smile at her skeptical appraisal. "It's me. I promise."

She seemed satisfied and opened the door to let him in. She kept her body behind the door, as though protecting herself from whoever might be following him.

As he stepped into the living room, she closed the door behind him, still using one hand to cover her left eye. Tears still streaked down her cheeks, but she didn't look as upset as when she first arrived.

Putting his hand on her upper arm and leading

her to the couch, he asked, "What happened to your eye?"

Her face crumbled. "I got something in it when my bike crashed into the ditch."

"Let me see," he said softly. Her ponytail was an untamed mess from the wild sprint through the woods, so he smoothed it down as best he could while trying to examine her eyes. She kept both hands over her left eye and her right closed so tightly that it puckered the delicate skin around it.

"It'll be all right," he whispered, still running his hand over her hair. "Please let me help you."

She flinched.

"Okay, here's what we're going to do," he said in as soothing a tone as he could make it. "You're going to sit here and keep your eye closed. I'm going to go find my first-aid kit and see if there's an eye wash kit with it."

She nodded cautiously.

A dash outside to the trunk of his car, and he found the box right where Heather had thrown it before he left Portland. Sure enough it had a professional-looking eye wash kit.

Kneeling before Danielle once again, he gently wrapped his fingers around her wrists. "I need to take a look now."

She nodded again, her breathing returning to a more even pace.

The pain was subsiding for the moment. But he'd change that as soon as he opened her eye.

Dear Lord, please let me be able to help Danielle without causing her too much more pain. Please let this just be a scratch and not something that needs major medical attention.

With steady hands he gently pulled her wrists away from her face and pushed them to her sides. Both eyes were still closed tightly and tears streamed from beneath the lashes of her left eye.

"All right. Here's what I'm going to do. First I'm going to open your eyelid and see if I can see whatever's in there. Then I'm going to try to get it out. When it comes out, then we're going to rinse your eye with the wash. Any questions?"

She shook her head, then stopped suddenly and said in a wavering voice. "What about my contacts?"

Contacts?

"Do you think you could take it out yourself?"

"No."

He looked at the label on the bottle again. It explicitly said to wash hands—dashing to the bathroom, he scrubbed his hands and hurried back to remove any contact lenses and surrounding eye makeup before rinsing. It didn't look like she was wearing any makeup, so the contact lenses were the only problem. Maybe this was beyond his brief first-aid expertise. He'd received a lot of training at Quantico, but he wasn't a medical expert by any stretch of the imagination.

"Then I'll take you to the hospital."

"No!" she yelled, grabbing his shirtsleeve in a vise grip and staring at him through her open eye. "Please."

"Okay. Do you trust me to do it then?"

"No." She took a shuddering breath. "But do it anyway."

He swiped his thumbs across her damp cheeks, tilting her head back slightly. "I'll make this as fast as I can. Just breathe deep and try not to jerk your head."

She mumbled something incoherent, sucked in another deep breath and clenched her jaw. In one swift motion, he pried her eyelids apart with one hand and used the pad of the forefinger of his other hand to brush the lens from her iris. The dark brown contact tore slightly as it jumped into his hand, so he flung it on the floor, immediately picking up the sterile eye washing kit. He fit the end over her eye and squeezed gently to get the flow started. Soon her face and shoulders were damp from the liquid, but the muscles in her neck began to relax.

"Hang in there. Almost done."

Moments later the bottle was empty, and Danielle looked a bit like a drowned rodent, one half of her hair sopping wet. When she lifted her head, her eye was still closed.

"Does it feel better?"

She nodded. "I think so."

"Can you open it for me?"

She did, and Nate nearly fell over.

It was pure gold. One of the golden eyes he'd seen in his case file.

NINE

How had Nate never noticed that Danielle's cheekbones were the same shape as his pictures of Nora? Why hadn't he noticed the same little cleft in her lower lip? How had he not seen that Nora—his assignment—had been right in front of him for days? At least he was ninety percent sure it was her. Sure, her hair had changed and her face was a little thinner. But now that he looked for the clues to her identity, they were all there.

"Did you find him?"

"Huh?" Nate blinked twice, trying to move his mind from his thoughts to hers.

"The man who chased me. You didn't find him, did you?" Her voice carried toward the ceiling as she rested her head against the back of the couch.

"No. I'm sorry." He jabbed his fingers through his hair and glared at the spot where his knees met the faded carpet.

First he needed to find out for sure if Danielle

was really Nora—without scaring her off. Then he needed to get her to the safe house, away from the Shadow and anyone else that wanted to use her to manipulate her father.

"It's okay," she sighed, leaning forward. Out of the corner of his eye, he saw her shift uncomfortably. Her face scrunched up in pain, and she immediately stopped all movement.

"What hurts?"

"Everything."

The chuckle that escaped was natural, and he realized that he'd been laughing a lot since meeting Danielle—Nora—or was it just Danielle?

He didn't even know how to think of her. He had to get this straightened out.

Shifting to the adjacent chair, he cleared his throat then looked into Danielle's eyes—both the brown and the gold. She frowned slightly. Could she sense his tension? He sucked in a quick breath and exhaled in a prayer for the right words to help her open up to him.

Resting his elbows on his knees, he leaned in just a bit. "Danielle, I need to tell you something." Her brows furrowed, but she nodded slowly. "I haven't been completely honest with you."

"What do you mean, Nate?" Danielle's breath vanished as she realized that she didn't know as much about Nate as she felt like she did. It was easy being around him, and she definitely felt safe with him. But was it an act? Had he been fooling her for days?

He rubbed his hands together like he was trying to start a fire, finally raising his gaze from the floor to meet hers. "I'm from—" his voice broke, and he paused for a moment to clear his throat. "Well, there's just no really easy way to say this...."

When he didn't continue, her heart sank, and she had to grab the couch cushion beside her leg to keep from jumping up and pacing the small room. "Tell me what's going on. Tell me now."

His Adam's apple bobbed once before he said, "I'm a special agent with the FBI. I'm here in Crescent City on assignment."

"You're FBI?" Her words felt forced, like they were coming from someone else's mouth, disconnected from her thoughts.

He nodded and quickly grabbed a small leather wallet from the end table. Flipping it open, he revealed a card and bronze badge that identified Nathan Andersen as an FBI special agent. She flipped it closed and handed it back to him, once again meeting his gaze—the uncertainty gone. His fingertips brushed hers, and he offered her a tentative smile.

"It's a terrible picture of you."

"Hey!" His voice was both subdued and full of mock indignation. He obviously knew what she knew. His handsome face and striking features were perfectly captured on the ID.

"Just kidding." She finally pulled her eyes from his gaze and looked down at her hands. Well, that certainly explained the gun that he'd surreptitiously slipped into the waistband of his jeans before pursuing the man who had chased her. What it didn't explain was why he was telling her.

"Why tell me?" she finally asked, when it was clear he wasn't going to continue.

He shrugged, his blue-gray eyes clear. "See, I've been working on this case for a couple of years now. I've been trying to nail this guy for money laundering, drugs, kidnapping, murder. I have a witness who's ready to testify and the case is pretty much closed. Just one hitch. The witness's daughter is being threatened."

It didn't make any sense. His story just didn't register. How did it relate to her? She shook her head and squinted, asking the question without speaking.

"The man who did those terrible things is Phil Goodwill."

Tears flooded her eyes, and she blinked furiously. Her emotions could be neither identified nor controlled.

"Do you understand what I'm saying?" Nate's hand was warm on her arm, as he leaned in. But she couldn't make herself speak. Her brain simply could not comprehend what his words meant. Her father was gone. He couldn't possibly be talking about her. He couldn't possibly know that she had a connection to Goodwill.

Could he?

Reaching for the deflated throw pillow, she hugged it to her chest. Just having something to hold gave her the courage to respond. In this case ignorance was not bliss. She had to know what he knew and what on earth was going on.

"Don't baby me. Just tell me what you know."

His hand squeezed her shoulder, and he said, "Danielle, is your real name Nora James?"

She hadn't heard that name in a year and a half, and it felt strange yet familiar like a long lost friend. "Nora James?" She rolled the name around her tongue for a moment, remembering the sound of her father's voice calling her for dinner. Her lips twitched, and for the first time, his memory brought joy mingled with regret.

She should have been able to save him. But she'd failed.

"You are Nora, aren't you?" he said, his words neither accusatory nor gentle.

She thought about lying for a split second, but his story didn't make any sense to her, and she needed to know what he was talking about. "Yes."

He leaned back and chewed on his bottom lip, closing one eye and evaluating her through the other. His arms crossed over his chest, but he remained silent.

"How did you know? How long have you known? What did you mean before about Goodwill? You're talking about me and my father? But what did you mean about my father's testimony? Did you depose him before he died or something?" The questions would have continued except that his posture suddenly straightened and a wrinkle formed between his eyes.

"What do you mean before your father died?"

"Before he died. Before that night in the alley."

He frowned, brushing at the unruly lock of hair covering his forehead. "Danielle, your dad's alive."

"No. I saw him get shot. My dad, Parker James, was shot—in the alley that night. I saw him fall. I saw the blood." Speaking the memory made her hands shake, and she clenched the pillow tighter.

Nate's expression changed from confusion to something she couldn't read. It was close to pity mixed with sadness. The corner of his lips raised in a grimace as he reached for her arm again, but stopped short. "Your dad was shot. But he made it. It was touch and go there for a while, but he's fine now."

The sob that escaped her throat sounded like it

came from someone else, and even her hand over her mouth didn't muffle the noise. "He's alive?"

A wide grin split Nate's face. "Yes. He's alive."

She jumped to her feet and threw her arms around Nate's neck, burying her face in the space between his shoulder and chin. He slowly wrapped his arms around her, patting her back intermittently. She inhaled deeply, drinking in the clean scent of his aftershave.

After several long seconds, he helped her back to the couch. "Let me get you some water." While he hurried to the kitchen, she wiped at the teardrops still clinging to her eyelashes.

Her dad was alive.

Thank You, God, for saving my dad. And thank You for bringing Nate into my life to tell me.

Nate returned, squatting in front of her and holding out a blue plastic cup. "Drink up."

She did as she was told, sucking the tepid water down in one gulp. Wiping her upper lip with the back of her hand, she let loose the smile she'd missed for so long whenever she thought of her dad. Oh, the time they'd missed together. She'd make it up.

"When can I see him? Can I call him?"

Nate didn't even miss a beat. "ASAP. I'll start making calls right away. We're going to get you to the safe house in Portland. You'll be with your dad in just a couple days."

"Really?"

"Really." He reached for his cell phone, flipping it open and speed-dialing his office. Pressing the phone to his ear, he whispered, "I just need to let them know we're coming back to Portland."

When someone on the other end of the line picked up, he turned and stepped into the kitchen. His words, muffled by the distance, didn't make any sense to her. Then again, maybe it wasn't the few yards into the kitchen. Her ears roared with the blood rushing through every inch of her. Everything she'd believed was false.

Suddenly her knees buckled, and she melted back onto the couch. Moisture collected in the corner of her eyes, and she folded over her knees, only able to send up a silent prayer of thankfulness over and over.

Her first indication that Nate had returned to the living room was the weight of his hand on her shoulder. "Danielle." He paused until she looked up into his face. "I know this is a lot."

That was the understatement of the century, and she could only manage to nod.

"Can I get you anything?" He pulled his hand back and passed his phone back and forth in front of Danielle. Her eyes followed it, as she thought about what she really wanted.

"I'd like to talk to my dad."

A grin unlike any she'd seen before split his features. "I think we can arrange that. Hold on just a second." He quickly dialed and waited for it to be answered. "Heather, it's Andersen. Danielle—I mean, Nora—wants to talk with her dad. Patch me through to the safe house?"

Seconds dragged by, and her stomach erupted with butterflies until it dropped to her toes at the same moment that Nate said, "Mr. James, this is Special Agent Andersen. I have someone here who would like to talk with you." He handed her the phone and pointed to the door, excusing himself.

Inhaling through her nose, Danielle cleared her throat before putting the receiver to her ear. "Dad?"

The person on the other end of the line sucked in a sharp breath. "Nora, sweetie? Is it really you?"

"Oh, Dad! I've missed you!" And then she couldn't control the sobs that wracked her body, choking on the desperate breaths. "Dad. Dad."

Just saying his name over and over seemed her only chance to confirm that it really was him. That this wasn't an elaborate hoax. He'd been lost to her, and now he had been returned.

A pang of guilt stabbed her middle.

She'd lost him because of her own fear. It was her own fault that she'd run. Her own fear of Goodwill had kept them apart for more than a year.

"Daddy, I'm so sorry."

"What are you sorry for? You haven't done anything wrong. This was my mess. I never meant for you to get involved." His voice was strong and soothing, just like she remembered it, but so unlike the last night she'd seen him.

"But—I—I ran away. I was so sc-cared." Swallowing hiccups hurt her chest, but she did everything she could to control her words. "I ran away and left you there. They shot you!"

His quiet laughter filled the line. "I remember."

"Oh, Dad! Are you okay?"

"Good as new. One little surgery, and the doctors say I'm better than ever." Moments of pure silence passed, and although she opened her mouth to speak, Danielle couldn't manage to get a word out. Finally her dad asked, "How are you doing? I've missed you so much."

"I've missed you, too," she managed to say before her throat closed up again, emotion clogged all hope of further speech.

"Listen, honey, they're telling me I have to go. They need to keep this line open. But they're bringing you here, right? Special Agent Andersen is bringing you here? Soon?"

"Uh-huh. I'll be there soon."

She hadn't noticed her hands shaking during the call, but once she hung up, she couldn't make them stop. Clasping them together didn't work, so she sat on them, fighting the rush of guilt that continued. No matter what her dad said, she knew that her fear had cost them dearly.

Replaying the conversation over and over in her mind kept her busy until Nate returned several minutes later. He slipped silently through the front door, locking it behind him.

"How was your call?"

She met his gaze through blurry eyes as she held his phone out to him. "Thank you."

He nodded, his neck stiff and awkward. Then he turned away slightly, speaking out of the side of his mouth. "No problem."

Danielle took it as her hint to get her emotions under control, so she knuckled away her tears and cleared her throat. "Okay, so when do we leave."

"Tomorrow. First thing."

"Good. Will we fly? Or drive?"

"We'll drive. That way we can go straight to the safe house, and it doesn't give Goodwill's people a chance to track us. Plus I have to return the Bureau's car."

That elicited a half smile. "True. I didn't put all that hard work into it just for you to leave it behind."

"We'll get back to Portland early the next morning."

"But why would Goodwill be watching the

airports for you? Or me?" Her eyebrows pinched together. "Wait. Does that mean…" A flash of his words from just minutes before played through her mind. "You said something before. You said your witness's daughter was being threatened. That's me. What's going on?"

He shook his head, as though debating how much to tell her. "What it means is that we need to get you to the safe house as soon as we can. And that means you'll be reunited with your father that much sooner."

He was trying to distract her. She could read it on his face.

"Nice try Special Agent Andersen." She reached out to him as though a physical connection might make him tell her the whole truth. "Please. I need to know. Is that why someone ran me off the road today?"

"It's possible that the two are related."

"Then I have a right to know."

He nodded, lowering himself to the floor and leaning his back against the base of the oversized chair. "We have a mole inside Goodwill's organization. That mole overhead a conversation… Wait. Let me back up. We've been looking for you for a year and half. When you sped out of that alley, we didn't have time to chase after you. Our concern obviously was saving your dad's life and arresting the man who shot him." He adjusted his seat, looking at the bare wall on the other side of the room. "We knew we had to find you, but you'd disappeared. We couldn't find any trace of you. You've done a good job of hiding. No pay checks. No credit cards. No housing applications. Nothing we could track."

She warmed at his compliment—of sorts. "Thanks. When I left Portland, I tried two other towns, but I couldn't find a place to stay long-term that didn't require a credit check. Andy literally rescued me by giving me a job and place to live. He takes out my taxes for me and pays me in cash. And he doesn't ask a lot of questions."

Nate smiled at that. "The mole wasn't able to get word on where you were. But Goodwill's organization was looking for you, too. Then, last week, we got word that a man Goodwill hired to find you had tracked you here. I came out here as soon as we got the word."

"And this man that tracked me down?"

"He's here, too."

She swallowed, her throat parched, the empty cup in her hand useless. "He's looking for me." It wasn't a question. She already knew the answer.

"Yes."

"What does he want with me? You already said you have everything you need to close your case against Goodwill." When Nate didn't move to answer, she offered her best guess. "Is he going to hold me ransom so that my father won't testify?" He looked surprised at her blunt statement. "Did you forget that I've already been kidnapped and ransomed by Goodwill's men once?"

She'd buried that experience along with the name Nora James, but owning the name meant owning the memory, too. So she ignored the chill that shook her from head to toe.

"No. I didn't forget." His hand shot through his hair, and his nose wrinkled.

"What if this guy fails? What if he doesn't get me? What's he supposed to do?"

"It doesn't matter. Once you're safe, your father can testify without having to worry about you."

He was dodging her questions again. "It does matter. It matters to me."

Nate sighed and rested his elbow on one bent knee. "Once we get you to the safe house, you and your dad will be protected. That's what's important. We'll protect you, and we won't let anyone hurt you or your father."

The truth lingered under his words, camouflaged by his promises and indirect answers. She squinted at him, playing his words over in her mind. What was he hiding?

"So what you're not saying is that when I disappear—when I go with you to the safe house—and Goodwill's guy can't find me—he's going to go after my dad to keep him from testifying?"

TEN

Nate's eyes darkened and a muscle in his jaw jumped. "Yes. But he's protected. Nothing is going to happen to him. He's safe."

"But how do you know?" Danielle asked, dread seeping from every pore.

He shook his head. "Portland is our turf. My team and I have it under control."

Her stomach lurched. She'd already lost her father once. She'd failed to save him, and she couldn't go through that again. Not when it was within her power to keep her father safe by focusing Goodwill's attention on her. She couldn't handle losing him again.

"I can't go. I'm sorry." Her lip quivered, and she bit it in an attempt to keep her emotions under control.

"What are you talking about? This isn't a negotiation." The tone of his voice was hard, immovable.

"I'm sorry. I won't exchange my life for my

father's. He risked his for mine, and I won't put him in danger again."

Was that pain crossing Nate's face? He looked away, his jaw clenching and unclenching as he rubbed his palm over his already mussed hair. Finally he shook his head. "You don't have a say in whether you go back to Portland or not. You're going. Period. End of story."

"Oh, Nate. Don't you see? As long as I'm out in the open, the man looking for me isn't after my dad." She implored him with her eyes. "We have to find this guy before he finds me or my dad. You and I have to do this. It's the only way we can keep my dad safe."

"But the FBI will keep him safe in Portland," Nate said, an underlying growl making his words more intense.

She hated her next move, but she was out of options. Nate wasn't going to give in, and she couldn't, either. There was no way she could live with the guilt of losing her father a second time when she had the power to protect him.

Keeping her tone as even as she could, she looked him in the face. "If you try to force me to leave Crescent City, I'm going to run away and leave enough clues that Goodwill's guy will know exactly where to go to follow me—away from my father."

"But that's blackmail."

"Yes it is. And I'm sorry."

"And what if you're found? You could be seriously injured or killed."

A tiny smile lifted her lips. "So wouldn't it be better if you and I look for this guy together? You can make sure that if he does find me, you guys can pick him up first. Isn't that a much better plan than me running off and maybe getting myself killed?"

He hung his head and closed his eyes.

She had him.

Nate rubbed his eyes with the heels of his hands, hoping the pressure would start to ease the pounding at his temples. Danielle—Nora—whatever she called herself, was going to get herself killed, and it was going to be on his conscience.

But she had him backed into a corner.

Resting his chin on his chest, he barely heard her stand. "May I use your restroom?"

He couldn't even find his voice to respond, just pointed at the door next to the bedroom. Her feet shuffled unevenly across the carpet. His head snapped up at her uneven steps, and he caught her last limping movement before she disappeared behind the closed the door.

During their twenty-minute argument, he'd somehow managed to forget that she'd been run off the road and chased through the woods.

Undoubtedly, this revelation of Danielle's true identity added a whole new level of danger to that situation. She was probably injured and definitely in trouble.

And somehow she was the first person he'd met in Crescent City. It wasn't a coincidence. Their paths had crossed for a reason. There had been a plan in place for Nate to protect Danielle from the beginning. And he intended to keep her safe. Regardless if she cooperated.

"Lord, save us both from our foolishness," he muttered, pushing himself to his feet. Water ran in the sink on the other side of the closed door as he headed into the kitchen. He needed coffee. Maybe the caffeine would help his head feel more normal.

He'd just finished setting up the coffee maker, when Danielle hobbled into the living room, heading for the couch.

"Which leg hurts?" he called, up to his elbow in the pit of his freezer, looking for a bag of vegetables.

She swallowed quickly. "They both do."

That brought a small chuckle. "Fair enough. Does one area hurt worse than the others?"

"My right ankle. I think I twisted it when I fell in the woods." Her eyes darted around the room, anywhere but at him, as he returned to stand before her.

"Let me take a look."

He knelt so he was practically sitting on his feet and slipped his hands around her right shoe. She winced slightly as he gently tugged. It didn't budge, so he loosened the laces and pulled again. The shoe barely moved. Her foot was probably pretty swollen. On his third try it popped off, and Danielle sighed softly, leaning back into the flimsy sofa cushions.

But when he gently grabbed the hem of the leg of her athletic pants, her entire body suddenly tensed.

"Does that hurt?"

She didn't say anything for a moment, as she cringed. "A little."

He looked up to meet her hooded gaze as he rolled her pant leg up several times. Danielle offered him a brave smile, and he returned a strong grin as he plopped the frozen peas on her ankle. Her eyes shot open and she yelped, kicking her left leg and catching his thigh.

He grinned, not offering any apologies.

Forehead wrinkled and hands clasped in her lap, she asked, "Are you angry with me?"

"Yes."

"I'm sorry."

Standing and putting his hands on his hips, he surveyed his case. She didn't look like much with a rip in her pants, a leaf in her hair, and two very different-colored eyes beneath fair lashes. But those eyes pleaded with him to understand.

And he did. To a point.

He felt for her, thinking that her dad had been dead for over a year. She'd lost all that time with him, and she hadn't known it until today. He wasn't going to change her mind with the logic of safety. Hers was an emotional reaction. And he couldn't afford to lose track of her if she ran off. It would be safer for her and Parker if he stuck with her—and did everything in his power to find the Shadow before he made his move.

"I know you are." He squinted at her one more time, then nodded. "I'm not going anywhere. You're stuck with me until we find Goodwill's man. Got it? Every minute, I want to know where you are."

She nodded, a tiny smile tugging at one corner of her mouth.

"So tell me everything you remember about what happened this morning."

She looked down at her ankle as though she was carefully studying the bag of peas resting there. When she lifted her eyes to meet his gaze, fear and trepidation had returned. "As I mentioned before, I had a flat tire this morning, and I really needed to stretch my legs. I needed to get out of the house. I was hurting all over from tossing and turning last night and I just wanted to get into the pool. I thought some exercise would help me relax and forget that there was someone in my house last night."

"What happened at the gym?"

She looked up at the ceiling as though trying to remember the details. "When I got there I went to the locker room then straight to the pool. I was only about halfway through my laps when someone jumped into my lane. It was Kirk."

"From class?"

"Same guy. He followed me when I got out of the pool."

The hairs on Nate's neck stood on end, and all of his senses jumped into overdrive. "Did he hurt you?" If he did, he was going to get a late-night visit from a very angry FBI agent. Nate wasn't going to stand by while some creep followed Danielle around. Even if he wasn't remotely convinced that Kirk was really the one he should be concerned about.

She laughed lightly, the sound a salve to his crackling nerves. "No—not at all. He just pestered me for some extra help in class. He seemed pretty desperate for some one-on-one time, but then said he isn't planning on coming to class on Tuesday. Ugh! I was so mad. I almost pushed him in the pool!"

Nate didn't bother trying to stop the laugh that burst out as Danielle's slender arms crossed over her chest and she huffed a lock of brown hair off her forehead, turning her face away from him. "Well, I almost did," she continued, as though his laugh implied that he didn't believe her.

"I'm sure you would have."

"I should have." She glanced down at him out of the corner of her eye, and he realized that he was still seated on the floor with her injured ankle resting lightly on his knee, but he didn't make a move to shift positions.

"So what happened after your run-in with Kirk? Did you see him again?"

"No. I just went back to the locker room, grabbed my bag and got on my bike to head back to the garage—the garage! Gretchen is going to be so worried! I have to call her."

Nate jumped to his feet and grabbed his cell phone, tossing it in her direction. She quickly dialed the number as he walked back into the living room.

When Danielle hung up, she looked much less panicked.

"Everything okay at the garage?" Nate asked.

"Yes. I told Gretchen I won't be coming in today. She's going to cover for me."

"Good. Now back to this morning—did you recognize anyone else at the gym?"

"Hmm…" She closed her eyes in deep thought. "Oh! Yes, of course. I ran into Ivey, too, before and after my swim. She was just doing the cross trainer or something. And Ridley literally ran into me in the hall." She paused. "Anyway, when I got onto my bike, I didn't think anything was wrong, but then I got going down that hill on Beeker Street, and I tried my brakes. They wouldn't work."

"At all?"

She shook her head, eyebrows tugged together. "Not at all. I looked down as quick as I could—considering that I was practically flying down the hill—and it looked like the brake wire had been cut. And then I noticed that I was being followed by a blue Ford Explorer."

"Did you get a license plate?" He found himself leaning forward, his elbows on his knees as he listened to her story.

She shook her head again. "It all happened so fast. One minute I was just pedaling home and the next I had no control over my bike. Even my handle bars felt loose. The next thing I knew I was making the decision to crash in the road or take the fall into the ditch." Her voice hitched as she recounted the terrifying incident. "The Explorer was on my tail and then pulling along beside me. I didn't have a choice, so I just cranked the handle bars into the ditch. Suddenly I was on my back with the wind completely knocked out of me.

"But when I tried to get up, the Explorer came back and I could see the jeans of someone standing on the road above me. I'm pretty sure that's who chased me through the woods."

Her breathing had quickened as she told the story, and fear pooled in her eyes once again. Nate reached out and grabbed her hand, holding it firmly in his steady grip. "Did you ever see the guy's face? Or any distinguishing features?"

"No."

"Did he ever call after you?"

"No. I don't think so."

Nate sorted that out in his mind. If Danielle's pursuer had meant no harm, he would have called to her, tried to get her attention. No, the man chasing her had definitely been after her in the worst sense of the word. But was it the Shadow trying to make his move? Would he be so reckless? Or was someone else pursuing her, too?

"Well, like I said, you and I need to stick close together. I'll do anything I can to protect you, but if I'm not with you, I can't keep you safe. I'll sleep in my car outside your apartment."

"Don't be ridiculous. We can set up an air mattress in the office. There's no need for you to sleep in your car."

"We'll just share meals and check in together. It won't be much different than now…except you'll spend every minute of the day with me."

"Fine. But if we're going to be sharing all of

these meals, are you going to cook for me?" she teased.

He smiled. "Sure."

"Just as long as you aren't going to cook up these peas and make me eat them." She laughed as she wiggled her toes, sending the bag of melting vegetables bouncing.

"Not for lunch, but I won't make any promises about dinner."

After lunch, Nate drove them to the scene of Danielle's crash. She couldn't help the way her eyes darted everywhere, looking for any sign of the blue SUV. But there was no indication that there had even been a car there.

There were, however, plenty of signs of her wreck. Her swimsuit and gray gym bag were just where they had fallen during her tumble. The two silver pieces that had once made up her cell phone lay next to her clump of a towel. Black flip-flops were on opposite ends of the debris, and smack in the middle was her bicycle—the front wheel irreparably damaged.

Just looking at the scene brought tears to her eyes. How had she ever escaped from that mess?

She stepped out of the car and walked around to the front of it, meeting Nate there. He slipped his arm around her waist, and she leaned into his shoulder. He seemed to just know that she needed to be held at that moment, and she took comfort in his solidity.

"Well, shall we go take a closer look?" he finally said after several moments of silence.

She inhaled deeply through her nose. He smelled like earth and coffee and comfort. "Okay."

Telling herself that she didn't want to trip on her sore ankle, she didn't let go of his hand as they stumbled into the ditch, but she had a sneaking suspicion that she liked holding his hand for a completely different reason. He felt like a lock that would never be broken. Like brakes that would never fail. Like safety.

Even if she couldn't keep the feeling in her life for the long-term, at this moment, it felt wonderful to feel safe.

When they reached the flat bottom of the ditch, Danielle lost her excuse for clinging to him, so she grudgingly let him wander in the direction of her bike. As he squatted to get a closer look, his jeans pulled tightly against his thigh and he rested an elbow on his knee. With his other hand he picked up the black rubber tubing of the bike's brake wire. She couldn't take her eyes off the way he moved with such power and purpose.

A fly buzzed by her ear, and she snapped out of her trance, deciding she should start picking up her things. She had just put her towel back in her bag when Nate finally spoke.

"It's definitely been cut."

"How can you tell?"

He motioned her over and pointed at the end of the tubing. "It's a clean cut. If this had broken on its own, there'd be a lot of fraying around the edge here. And it's likely the rubber never would have been severed—at least not completely. Someone did this on purpose. And they were smart about it, too." He gestured with his hand. "See where they cut it? It's right next to the brake, so that you wouldn't notice it just by glancing at the bike. You wouldn't notice until you tried pulling on your brakes."

She quivered with a fresh wave of uncertainty. How could someone be so cruel? Goodwill's man was just plain evil.

"Let's grab your things and go back to your place."

Danielle nodded silently, at a complete loss for words.

When she stooped down to pick up the larger piece of her phone, an enormous, ugly toad jumped at her. She shrieked and stumbled backward, landing heavily on her rear.

Nate was by her side in an instant. "You okay?" he asked.

She blinked rapidly as he held his hand out in front of her. His stance was solid, as though braced to pick her up if she needed it. At the very least he offered her a tug to get her back on her feet.

She grabbed at his hand, but he deftly dodged her fingers, instead wrapping his hand completely around her wrist. His tug was swift, and she popped to her feet, nearly toppling over onto him. Nate caught her shoulders and ducked down to look into her eyes, but she evaded his gaze, struggling to get sudden wayward tears under control. How could she possibly be breaking down at this moment? She was next to the strongest man she'd ever met, and she felt like she was falling apart.

"Hey… Danielle." Nate put his fingers on her chin and turned her face back so that he could look into her eyes. "It's going to be okay. We're in this together. Okay?"

She could only manage a small nod.

Suddenly his kindness was too much. His gentle touch and sweet words stole her energy. She'd been trying so hard to keep everything together, but at that moment, she crumbled into his arms, tucked her head under his chin and didn't worry about the tears trekking down her cheeks. And he just wrapped his arms around her and held on tight. She could hear his heart beating, and she pressed a little closer. The soft cotton of his T-shirt felt like her pillowcase, and she could almost fall asleep standing there.

Softly he began whispering into her hair, but

she couldn't make out all of his words. "…Please keep Danielle safe… We trust in You…comfort Danielle now… Help us to find this man, and show us where to look… Amen."

When he stopped praying, he held her for just a little while longer, then finally stepped back, keeping her at arm's length. She was glad he kept his hands wrapped around her shoulders, but not because she was afraid of collapsing again. She was suddenly filled with strength in the very spot where God had bolstered her just that morning, and she sent up another prayer of thanksgiving.

"Let's get a move on," Nate said. "I'll grab your bike. Can you get the rest of your stuff?"

"I think so." He turned, but she effectively stopped him with just a gentle brush of her hand on his arm. "Thank you."

"You're welcome." His nod was brief as he excused himself, and he quickly moved to pick up her bike.

He was halfway back to the car by the time Danielle finally got her feet to move. She scurried to pick up the rest of her things and met him back at his car just as he closed the trunk. He opened the passenger's side door for her then walked around the front of the sedan and quickly slid in beside her.

His eyebrows were pulled together, and he looked suddenly very solemn.

"What is it?" she asked after several long moments of silence.

"This is serious."

"I know." Her head tilted toward the ditch and the scene of her crash. She knew better than anyone the gravity of the situation.

His eyes followed her closely as he maneuvered them back onto the road and toward the garage. "Who had access to your bike while you were at the gym?"

"I don't know. Everyone, I guess. I locked it in the bike racks right by the front door."

He strummed his fingers on the steering wheel, eyes focused on the road in front of them. "Do you happen to know if your gym has security cameras?"

She shrugged. "I'm not sure."

"No problem. I'll call them today and see if they have anything that might be useful for us."

His body moved almost as if on autopilot as he parked his car by the side of the garage and got out. She hurried to join him as he stalked toward the door of her living quarters, his face an indecipherable mask. Immediately he jiggled the handle, the lock stuck in place, and he waited for her to open it.

When she did, he said, "Stay here." He reached to the back of his waistband and pulled his handgun from its place, sweeping through the rooms the way he had the night before. Just a moment later he returned, a slightly lighter look on his face. "It's safe."

She stepped past him and was halfway through her living room before she realized that he wasn't following her. "Nate?" she said, turning slowly.

"You'd best get some sleep. Your adrenaline is probably already fading, and you'll be asleep shortly. I'll hang out with Gretchen in the lobby. Come get me when you wake up."

He moved to close the door, but she hurried to stop him. He looked upset with her, but she couldn't go to bed without knowing that they were okay.

"Are you still angry with me?"

He shook his head.

"Please. I can tell you're upset. What is it?"

An emotion flickered across his face. It wasn't anger, but she couldn't easily identify it. His lips pursed to one side, and she took a half step closer.

They were barely two feet apart, and she leaned in just a little closer, seeking out that same strength that he'd shared just minutes earlier in the ditch. He was right. Her body was already shaking from the day's emotional tumult, and she was exhausted.

"Please," she whispered.

He looked down, then his piercing blue-gray

eyes met her gaze. "It's not you. It's me. This is all just… It's more than it's supposed to be."

"I don't understand."

His snort was thick with emotion. "That makes two of us."

She just didn't get it. How had she upset him again? He was still courteous, but there was something heavy about his demeanor. She had to know.

When he tried to turn from her again, she turned with him and stepped closer until she could feel his breath on her face. She put her hands on his shoulders and lifted herself up to her tiptoes. An inch away from his lips, she could sense the tension coursing through his muscles. His arms tightened under her fingers, but he didn't push her away. He didn't move back.

Instead he stepped toward her, closing the gap between them, pressing his mouth to hers and holding her tightly.

His lips were soft and reassuring as he deepened their connection, and she sighed into him, knowing that this was what she'd been longing for all day. She savored every bit of comfort that he offered, wiping away thoughts of the untamed terror of that morning.

As his strong hands turned circles on her back, she thought she'd never felt so safe.

Her eyes cracked open for an instant, and she

saw that his eyes were closed, an expression of peace on his face. She leaned closer, relishing in the moment.

Suddenly he pulled back, his features taut and eyes shadowed. "You'd better get some sleep. I'll see you later." He closed the door on her, and she could hear his heavy footfalls move around the building.

As she crawled into her bed without even changing her clothes, a lump rose to her throat. They could never be. He knew, and she did, too. After this assignment and Goodwill's trial they'd part ways. This case would always hang over their relationship—well, it wasn't really even a relationship.

And it wasn't likely to change.

ELEVEN

Nate awoke with a start, anger rushing through his veins. Anger at the situation—how could he not know who was after Danielle? Anger at himself—how could he take advantage of her vulnerability, especially with his track record?

He'd woken up in this same chair in the waiting room at Andy's before. The first time, he'd just been tired, grumpy. Now he was downright furious with himself for his actions. But both times he was running on a severe lack of sleep.

He'd gotten up every hour on the hour all night Friday and last night to walk around the property. Checking for a phantom blue SUV had kept him awake and forced him to think about his actions. To analyze the way Danielle felt in his arms and the feel of her lips against his. It had been nearly forty-eight hours since their kiss, but he could still remember every detail.

"Lord, I'm so sorry," he grumped into his hands that covered his face. "I don't know what got into me. I can't believe I lost control like that. I refuse to treat women like my dad and grandpa did. I can control my actions, and I won't lead Danielle on like I did Georgia. I don't want to hurt her. Help me to serve You and not to fail in this assignment."

When he finally lifted his head, his temples pounded, and his whiskers rubbed roughly against his palms. He needed a shower and a shave to feel human again. And at least half a gallon of coffee. It just didn't seem very likely at the moment.

But it was Sunday! Danielle would be going to church, and he'd definitely go with her. He couldn't go to church in his current state. Eyeballing his wrinkled jeans and T-shirt, he shook his head. He didn't even need a mirror to know that he was unacceptable.

As he exited the front office, locking the door with the key that Gretchen had given him the evening before, the sun was just beginning to peek over the horizon and a brisk wind chilled him slightly.

He hurried to Danielle's door and knocked softly. If she was awake, he didn't want to scare her. If she wasn't, he would knock louder the next time.

Several seconds passed.

He had just lifted his hand to knock again when he heard a small voice on the other side. "Who is it?" Good girl.

"It's just me. Nate."

The door opened a crack, and Danielle's head poked into the opening, her body completely hidden behind the wood. Her straight brown hair wild from sleep and eyes dazed, she looked like she'd just woken up. And absolutely beautiful.

Nate! Don't even let your mind go down that road.

"How'd you sleep?"

"Fine," she said around a large yawn.

"Good. I'm going to take one more walk around the property. Then I'm going to go home and get ready for church. What time should I pick you up?"

"Umm…" She closed one eye as though thinking hard about the question. "I guess eight forty-five."

"Okay—I'll see you then. Call me if you hear or see anything unusual. And don't answer the door for anyone else until I come back."

She nodded and closed the door. He waited until he heard the deadbolt click into place then quickly jogged around the building's perimeter.

When he was satisfied that she was safe for the time being, he jumped into his car and headed toward his apartment. With his phone on speaker, he called Heather's cell, which went straight to voicemail. "Heather, can you do me a favor and check on any blue Ford Explorers registered to Kirk Banner or Ridley Grant in the state of Colorado? Also, check for any that might belong to family members, even extended family. Call or text as soon as you have anything."

He hung up just as he pulled into his parking spot.

Jogging up the stairs to his landing, he almost made it inside his apartment before his neighbor from across the hall—the one whose door Danielle had pounded on a couple days before—stepped out. She was a kid, probably no more than twenty-two, but he had a sneaking suspicion that she kept her eye out for him. A lot.

Just now she sized him up with a gaze from head to toe and back, a longing look in her eyes. He cringed at her desperation. He knew he wasn't anything special to look at. Not the scum of the earth or anything, but he certainly wasn't a movie star, especially with his wrinkled clothes, wild hair and overnight beard growth.

"Morning," he said, nodding in her direction. It never hurt to be polite.

"You, too." Her smile was wide and revealed a row of slightly crooked teeth.

"See you later."

She waved a hand that was covered by the sleeve of her gray sweatshirt. She pursed her lips in an unattractive grimace, and he couldn't help but think about how Danielle looked so cute when she shot him a similar expression.

Ugh. He had to get his mind off Danielle.

Even as he turned his back on the girl and stepped into his home, he could feel her eyes boring a hole into his back. He withheld the urge to let loose a shudder as he clicked the lock into place.

He leaned his back against the door and surveyed his place. It was still just this side of being a rat hole, but somehow it had become his rat hole, and the thought brought a smile to his face. Even if it was temporary, it was just good to be somewhere that he could call his own. A place with real furniture to relax on, not plastic chairs.

He tossed his keys on the end table and headed into the kitchen. He flicked open the freezer and pulled out a bag of ground coffee from where it rested on a bag of frozen peas. He was halfway through pouring water into the coffee maker, when his brain clicked on. Something was definitely off.

He flung the freezer door back open, his gaze settling on the bag of peas that he'd used on Danielle's ankle on Friday. The problem was that he had tossed it into the freezer just before they headed over to the scene of her crash. He'd tossed it on top of his coffee. And he hadn't been home for more than a minute since then.

No way had the two bags been reversed without some help.

The realization sent him scrambling for his gun, which was still tucked into the shoulder holster under his jacket. He took his time moving room to room, checking to see if anything else was out of place. Everything looked okay until he came upon the pile of junk mail coupons on his nightstand. He distinctly remembered that the blue envelope with information on his apartment had been on the bottom of the stack. Now it was tucked in the middle.

He'd definitely had a visitor.

But who?

He walked to the sliding door that led to the private balcony off of his living room. The "private" part was a bit of a joke. It actually connected to his neighbor's with a half wall of flimsy wood. Anyone could have jumped from one to the other, and if the shuffled footprints in the dirt-covered cement were any indication, they had.

He squatted down and took a closer look at the imprints. They were shuffled enough that he couldn't tell an approximate shoe size or any distinguishing marks about them.

But he knew enough.

Someone thought he was a threat.

Danielle settled into a soft chair at First Church of Crescent City, the familiar seat a welcome haven from the unsettling recent events in her life. She closed her eyes amid the hustle and bustle of the sanctuary and said a silent prayer of thankfulness. For her dad and his return to her life. For her protection. For her life in Crescent City, no matter how disrupted it had become.

Even for Nate Andersen.

What she wasn't thankful for were the disturbing feelings that erupted every time he was near.

When she opened her eyes, she expected to see Nate standing in front of her. He'd said he was running back to the car for his bible. But she had a sneaking suspicion that he was checking on something else and definitely waiting for a call from Heather. He'd checked his phone every thirty seconds on the drive into downtown, and he'd been markedly silent during the trip. She'd been lost in her own thoughts of the previous several days, so she hadn't minded.

When her mind returned to the present and she actually opened her eyes, it wasn't Nate standing before her. It was Ivey.

"Hello!" the other woman greeted her.

"Ivey, so great to see you! I had no idea you go to church here."

Ivey shrugged her shoulder gently. "I've just started coming with a friend, but she couldn't make it this week." Her eyes drooped and a bit of the joy from her face disappeared.

"Would you like to join me? I'm also sitting with

a friend. He'll be here in a second. But you're more than welcome, as well."

Ivey's smile returned full blast, and she nodded enthusiastically. "I'd love to. Thanks!" She quickly walked around the edge of the pew and arranged her flowing pink skirt as she sat down next to Danielle. "Are we still planning for a little extra tutoring on Tuesday night?"

"Absolutely. I think I'll do some prep work for the class tomorrow, then I'll be all yours before class on Tuesday. Do you think an extra hour will be enough?"

"Oh, that should be plenty. Thanks again. I really—"

Danielle's head whipped around to see what had caused Ivey to stop talking and look so flabbergasted. Expecting Nate, she was again shocked to see Ridley Grant standing in freshly pressed khakis. He ran his hand over his immaculately styled hair and shot her a smirk.

"Well, well. Ms. Keating. Funny seeing you here." The way he said it, it didn't sound funny at all. It just made tremors run down her spine. "Mind if I join you ladies?"

"Actually—"

"Great." Ridley was seated next to her before she could say that Nate was out at the car and would be right back. He sat so close that when she inhaled, she nearly choked on the cloud of cologne hovering around him. But when she leaned a bit closer to Ivey seeking breathable air, he just leaned closer to her, making her both angry and uncomfortable.

She opened her mouth to tell him that Nate was on his way, but the words that caught the attention of their entire row weren't from her.

"Excuse me. You're in my seat." The voice was deep and low. Nate's eyes flashed dark gray like the steel in his voice. His broad shoulders filled out the dark blue button-up shirt that had made his eyes look so intense that morning when he picked her up, and he dwarfed Ridley's smaller frame, towering over him as he sat.

Ridley jumped to his feet, looking like he wasn't going to budge. But even standing, Nate had a solid three inches and twenty pounds of muscle on the guy. He didn't stand a chance.

Apparently Ridley thought the same thing, because he quickly ducked his head and mumbled a quick excuse before hightailing it down the center aisle.

Nate watched him go, then turned his gaze back to Danielle. With a small quirk of one of his eyebrows, he asked two questions: *What's he doing next to you? Are you all right?*

Fighting the urge to shrink away from his powerful stare, she offered a minimal shrug and a quick nod in response.

He seemed satisfied, so he quickly shook hands

with Ivey and then settled into the pew next to Danielle. While he was several inches farther away from her arm than Ridley had been, Nate caused goose bumps to break out on her skin. She rubbed her upper arms quickly, trying to regulate her body's reaction.

"Are you cold?" His breath was warm in her ear, and the quakes that danced down her spine were the opposite of the ones that Ridley had just given her. She didn't like either kind.

"I'm fine. Where's your bible?"

He looked at his empty hands and gave her a guilty grin. "Guess I forgot it. We'll have to share."

And share they did. After singing several contemporary worship songs and an old hymn, they sat back down and the pastor stood behind the pulpit, teaching about God's power on display when humans are at their weakest. Danielle tried valiantly to pay attention to his words, but Nate's arm resting on the back of her chair around her shoulders was quite distracting.

Of course, it was easier for him to lean in to read along from the bible she held in her hands without his arm in the way. But the feeling of it around her back was almost too intimate. Too comfortable. Like they'd been married for years and there was nothing more natural in the world.

She couldn't remember ever wishing for a church

service to hurry up and end, but the sensations Nate evoked made her focus far too much on her reaction to him. Didn't he feel it? Couldn't he tell that just his presence made her stomach swim?

She closed her eyes and bowed her head and tried to block out everything he made her feel. And like a friend's gentle embrace, she fell into silent prayer.

Dear Lord, what am I going to do? I can't have these feelings for Nate. I just can't. Just by being with me, he's in danger, and I hate that. He's trying to protect me, but what happens when the assignment is done? Will I ever really be safe and free from Goodwill? I can't stand to put Nate in danger forever.

And would you please take away this fear that keeps hovering over me? This knowledge that at any moment Goodwill's man is going to make his move. Keep Nate and I safe until this time is over. And please let me find peace with having to say goodbye to him when this is all over. But maybe I could have both? Both security and Nate? Both safety and love?

Love? Where did that come from?

Her mind went around and around trying to pinpoint the moment that she might have realized that she possibly loved Nate. Affection sure. She certainly felt plenty of that for him. Care. Concern.

An electric chemistry. She definitely liked him. A lot. But love?

No way. She'd done what she could to keep her distance. She had to for his sake. It couldn't be love. Could it?

Butterflies took control of her stomach and she wrapped her arm around her middle to quell them.

At that exact moment, Nate's elbow brushed hers as he brought his arm back to his side, drawing her into the present and back to the sermon. Or to be more precise, the benediction. Nate and Ivey stood on either side of her as the pastor prayed and the service ended.

Chatter started around her, but she could barely focus, so she stayed seated and took several very long seconds to gather her purse and join the discussion.

"So what are you two doing for lunch? Would you like to join me at Oregano Pete's? My treat."

Nate didn't say anything, so Danielle cleared her throat and offered a chipper, if distracted, "I love Oregano Pete's. They have the best cheesy garlic bread."

Nate put his arm around her shoulders again and squeezed just enough to get her attention. "Thanks for the invitation, Ivey. Maybe another day. We already have other plans."

"We do?" She barely kept her voice from

sounding as shocked as she felt. Since when was Nate making plans for them without telling her?

Nate nodded decisively. "Thanks again, though. See you in class on Tuesday."

"Sure thing." Ivey waved and strolled gracefully toward the foyer.

"What's going on?"

"We need to talk." His eyes darted around the emptying sanctuary. "But not here."

"Just tell me what's going on," she insisted.

The intensity in his eyes ramped up as he held her gaze. "There are three blue Explorers in the parking lot. I'm betting that one of them is the one that chased you down."

TWELVE

Nate was stumped. He had no idea where this case was going. More important, he had no idea who was involved.

He knew he and Danielle were at the center. But who was the third person? Was there a fourth that he wasn't even looking for?

He rolled onto his side on the air mattress he'd picked up after church the day before. On the tile floor of the waiting room at the shop, it wasn't the most comfortable bed he'd ever slept on. But it was certainly a step up from the shop's awful plastic chairs which he'd been using until now. At least he'd been able to sleep between his hourly trips around the building.

Again there had been nothing obvious to concern him. No cars. No tire tracks. No footprints.

He was still empty-handed and just about ready to chew nails, he was so angry with himself. He'd hoped that he and Danielle would get out of church fast enough to see who got into those three Explorers the day before. He'd even considered staying outside the entire service just to see who was driving them. But that would have left Danielle in the service by herself. He couldn't be sure that she was safe anywhere. Not even in a sanctuary. So he hurried back inside, hoping to catch the drivers leaving the building.

Of course, when he got back to his seat and saw it occupied by Ridley, he was more than grateful he hadn't found a hiding place around the corner of building just to scout out the parking lot. A wave of protectiveness washed through him in a way that he'd never experienced. He belonged next to Danielle, and he recognized that. Ridley was a jerk and belonged as far away from her as possible.

Sitting next to her in church, his arm around her shoulders was exactly what it should have been. Perfect.

Except that he shouldn't care for her as more than an assignment.

He smashed the heels of his hands into his closed eyes and he sank a little deeper into the mattress. Remembering the way that she looked with her short, dark hair gleaming in the morning sun—and her ripe-strawberries smell—made his head spin.

"But she's not yours to think about like that!" he growled at himself. He had to get his thoughts under control.

"But at least she doesn't think of me as more…" He let out a frustrated breath, taking solace in the knowledge that Danielle wasn't as attached to him as he was quickly becoming to her. He couldn't pretend his own feelings weren't involved. But as long as his heart was the only one on the line, he couldn't hurt her. He just had to make sure it stayed that way.

Besides, he was really just upset that they'd missed the driver of one of the Explorers. Another belonged to a nice little family with three kids. Quite certainly not the Shadow. But the last SUV had sat in the back corner of the parking lot until every other car in the lot had cleared out. Its owner never claimed it. Never drove it home.

He had a sneaking suspicion that it was parked there to taunt them.

And he still had no clue who he was looking for.

Suddenly his entire leg started vibrating, and he almost jumped off of the mattress, tumbling onto the hard tiles. He squirmed and wrestled until he dug his phone out of the cargo pocket of his khakis.

"Andersen," he croaked, his voice rusty from disuse.

"Boss. It's Heather."

He rolled to a seated position, instantly alert. "What do you have for me?" He flicked a quick glance at his watch. It was barely 7:30 a.m., which meant it was only 6:30 in Portland. She had some good news. Well, at least some news.

"I ran those plates from the three Explorers that you asked me to yesterday. Let's see." Papers rustled on the other end of the line, and he tried to collect every ounce of his patience. "Oh, here it is. The first is registered to James Dinofrio. No priors. His check is clean." That was probably the family he had seen. "The second is registered to George McFarland, but it's been reported as stolen."

"Of course it has." He shook his head in frustration. He couldn't catch a break in this case.

"But get this. The third is registered to a Mr. Kirk Banner."

"Really?"

"Yeah. I called you as soon as I found out. I figured you'd want to know right away."

A slow smile crept across his face. "Any chance Mr. Banner is our guy?"

"Doubtful."

The smile disappeared, and with it the hope that had started to rise in his chest. When the line was quiet for several seconds, he prodded Heather. "Because?"

"Oh," she replied. "Sorry, I was trying to multi-task and read e-mails. Things are pretty crazy right now. There's just no way Banner is the Shadow. Or even an accomplice. Goodwill would never have someone like him on payroll with this much at stake." She took a breath. "He has a couple priors. Small-time B and E, petty theft as a juvenile and one assault charge. That kind of thing. He's done a pretty poor job of covering his tracks. If he were on Goodwill's team—even if he wasn't the best man—his background wouldn't have been so easy to put together."

Nate didn't try to cover his sigh of annoyance. "And you're sure the Kirk Banner that owns the Explorer is the same one in the class at the college?"

"He's changed his hair color, but his face is the same on his driver's license and in the pictures you sent over."

"What about Ridley Grant? Anything on him yet?"

"Nope. I'm still looking, but so far nothing."

"Thanks for letting me know. Anything else?"

She paused for a few seconds, and he knew she was trying to weigh her words carefully. "I ran a facial scan on the pictures that you sent just to see if it picked anything up. It didn't identify anyone. I'm sorry."

"Me, too," he muttered. It had been a long shot, but any little break might help their case.

He grunted as he pushed himself up from the floor. Well, it was good to know that Kirk wasn't their guy. But why his fascination with Danielle?

And if it wasn't Kirk, Nate was coming far too close to running out of suspects before he found his man.

Coffee. He needed coffee.

Running his hands over the stubble on his face, he stretched his neck, trying to relieve the kinks. Grabbing his keys from the floor next to the bed and his gun from under the mattress, he headed out of the office, locking the door behind him.

He made one more circle of the property and was almost ready to head back to his apartment, when he noticed two sets of tire tracks in the dirt between a pair of shrubs near the east side of the gravel yard. Squatting down to take a closer look, he pulled out his phone and took a quick picture. One set of tracks was narrow and looked like it had come from a sedan or coupe of some sort. The other had a wide wheel base and wide tires. Definitely a truck or SUV. He'd bet it was from an Explorer.

His head snapped around, expecting to see the offending cars, but he was alone.

"God, this is not going well," he lamented up at the empty morning. "I'm doing a terrible job of protecting Danielle, and I'm falling short in every area of this investigation. I hate failing. Please help me."

He hung his head and rested his forearms on his knees, letting the silence envelop him. He waited, as if expecting an audible response from the heavens, but he heard nothing.

Okay, then. It was time to get the day started.

He couldn't keep Danielle safe for much longer without finding out who was in town determined to make her disappear for good.

Danielle rubbed her eyes with her fists, trying to clear the dancing spots from her line of vision. The pounding on her door continued as she tripped over the corner of her end table and fell heavily into the door.

"Danielle? Are you okay?" Nate's voice was filled with concern. When she rubbed the sore spot on her forehead instead of answering him, he jiggled the locked door handle and yelled louder. "Danielle! Answer the door now!"

"I'm here. I'm here," she grumbled as she unlocked the door and squinted at him through the pain that radiated through her entire skull. She pulled the lapels of her fluffy robe closer together, even though they already met under her chin.

Relief flashed across his face, followed quickly by concern and something more than worry. Was it fear?

He blinked and shook his face clear of emotion before she could really tell what was on his mind. "You hurt?" he finally asked, reaching out his thumb to tenderly touch her forehead, right where she'd plowed into the door.

Great. It had definitely left a mark.

"No—I just tripped." She took a half step back from him, trying to tear her gaze away from the overnight shadow that covered his face. His beard was a little darker than the rest of his hair, and when he grinned at her out of the corner of his mouth, he looked like every terrible rogue she'd ever read about and imagined in real life.

Except he wasn't a rogue.

He squinted his gray-blue eyes at her. "You sure?" Clearly, he didn't believe her.

Squaring her shoulders, she looked right into his eyes. "Yes. I'm fine. Now what on earth has you banging on my door at—" she spun to look at her clock "—seven thirty in the morning?"

"I need to go back to my apartment. I've got to get some coffee and get more than an hour of sleep at a time."

"Okay. Sounds good. Call me when you wake up." She moved to close the door, but something flashed through his eyes, making her stop. "What?"

He cleared his throat. "I found a couple sets of tire tracks in the dirt on the edge of the parking lot. They weren't there last night or anytime I walked around during the night. Someone was here between six-thirty and seven-thirty."

"Two sets? Were they—was one from…?" She couldn't bring herself to ask the question she really needed to know.

And Nate knew it. "Yes. I'm pretty sure one was from an Explorer."

She swallowed thickly, clinging to the door for support. Nate reached out and held her elbow gently until the strength in her legs returned. But her head didn't stop spinning. That blue Explorer had seemed so far away after her accident three days before. Even seeing the SUVs in the parking lot at church the day before hadn't seemed quite real. They could belong to anyone. She had nothing to fear from faceless car owners at her church. But faceless car owners in her own parking lot?

That was too close for comfort.

"What are you going to do?"

He dipped his head close to her ear, his breath tickling her neck. "I'm going to take care of you. You're safe. You're going to get ready for the day." There was a reassuring note to his voice that drove her fear away. "You're going to work in the garage with the bay door closed as long as Gretchen is here. I'll be back before she leaves for lunch."

His lips pressed softly against her cheek, and she leaned in to him, turning her head slightly, so that the corners of their mouths met for the briefest moment.

"Do me a favor," he said when he quickly pulled

back, a half smile playing on his face. "Don't leave your apartment until Gretchen is here."

"I won't." She managed a smile in return as he walked backward to his car.

"Lock the door," he called just before closing his own door.

Danielle did as she was told, slumping back against the hard wood, her chin pressed against her chest. Oh, this day had not started well. Not at all.

How on earth did Nate expect her to go about her normal day when someone had been in her parking lot that morning? When someone had been watching her home—while she was sleeping.

She sank to the floor, pressing her hands over her face.

Technically Nate knew how to keep her safe. But sometimes, when he kissed her, she worried that she was in more danger from losing her heart to him than she was from Goodwill's man. She couldn't deny her attraction to him, even if her head knew it couldn't be.

"Dear God, I'm so lost right now. I'm just so scared. I thought I'd be safe. I thought I'd come here and be free. I thought I'd be strong enough to do this on my own. I was supposed to be able to start a new life, to start over. But it's just not working out that way. Ahh!" Frustration flowed

as she clenched her fists, her heart racing. "Lord
please. Please. Help me."

When her pulse returned to normal, she pushed
herself to her feet. Trudging to her bedroom, she
did her best to make herself presentable for the day
masking the bags beneath her eyes and running a
brush through her tangled hair.

Gretchen arrived early, so Danielle joined her in
the office for several minutes before disappearing
into the garage beneath the hood of an old Chevy
But the work that she usually lost herself in so
easily wasn't doing anything to distract her from
the blue Explorer, its mystery driver and the set of
tire tracks on the outskirts of the property. Time
and again her mind's eye replayed the SUV on the
road as she biked home from the gym. She saw
the crash and physically felt the breath leaving her
body. She saw her cell phone smashed, the contents
of her gym bag sprawling the width of ditch.

And none of it compared to the terror she had
felt fleeing from the man chasing her through the
woods.

Her hands began shaking violently, and she
rubbed them together in an attempt to still her
nerves. Taking a deep breath, she picked up a
screwdriver, clenching it tightly in her right hand
By a sheer force of will, she managed to control
it enough to fit the Phillips-head into the slot of
the screw she needed to loosen, but turning it was

nother story. Even with both hands, she couldn't muster the strength to turn it a complete rotation.

"Danielle."

The voice was quiet, but so unexpected that she jumped, banging her head on the underside of the car's hood, the sound of vibrating metal engulfing her. She clasped a hand over the throbbing bump already forming before turning to look at her visitor.

Nate was already halfway to her, concern washing over his rested, shaven and very handsome face. "I'm sorry. I didn't mean to scare you."

"Uh-huh," she managed, even as her brain pounded in pain.

His hand rested gently on her upper back, and she had to fight both the urge to pull away and the one to lean closer into his arms. His eyebrows pulled together, as though he was deep in thought, but when he spoke, his voice was gentle. "Have you had lunch yet?"

"It's not time yet."

He simply held out his watch to her. It was nearly two o'clock. Where had her morning gone? And as if on cue, her stomach growled.

"Let's go get some lunch, then I'll take you over to the school and you can do some prep for tomorrow's class."

"All right." Looking down, she realized that the blue coveralls she wore weren't doing anything for her figure. Not that she wanted to be decked out in her cutest outfit, but Nate looked fresh and clean in his dark jeans and green sweater. She couldn't exactly get gussied up to go work in the classroom, but she could certainly do better than the shapeless tent. "Let me just go and get changed."

She changed clothes in record time, offered Gretchen a brief explanation and met Nate at his car. He was staring in the direction of the tire tracks as she approached, but he quickly turned his attention to her.

"So where to for lunch? Chinese?"

"Ohh...that does sound good." A smile actually lifted her cheeks. "I know the waiter at The Panda, Chan Chan. He's great."

"Chan Chan and The Panda it is, then." Nate returned her smile as he slid behind the wheel and started the car.

Sure enough, when they arrived at the restaurant, Chan Chan greeted them with his typical jubilance. "Your usual table, Danielle?"

"That'd be great. Thanks."

She'd hoped that orange chicken, egg drop soup, an egg roll and a wonton would take her mind off of the rest of her life, but as she spooned the first taste of soup into her mouth, she knew it wasn't going to work. This fear she had come to know would be in her life until...well, until it wasn't anymore. Until Goodwill's man was caught or he caught her.

The thought made her stomach roll.

On the other side of the booth, Nate seemed to take notice and caught her in his blue-gray gaze. Concern flickered across his face, but suddenly disappeared. "So what are you hoping to do in the classroom today?" His words were light and they matched his suddenly relaxed posture. He acted like he didn't have a care in the world, a half grin tugging up one side of his mouth.

She had a sneaking suspicion he was trying to distract her from the weight of the world on her shoulders, and she appreciated it. Indulging him, she went into detail about making sure that she had extra brake pads and shoes laid out for everyone for the next class.

Like a flash the afternoon disappeared, and they arrived at the college. The parking lot was empty except for the enormous trash bin at the end farthest from the building.

"How long do you think you'll be?" Nate asked, pulling into a parking spot.

"I don't know. Maybe an hour or so."

"Sounds good." They both got out of the car and headed toward the large brown doors. He walked her all the way to the entrance of her class-room, letting her unlock it before he said, "Let me just take a quick look around. Wait here." As he disappeared into the room, she saw him reaching for the gun tucked beneath his sweater.

It was the first time that afternoon that he morphed into special-agent mode. He'd done such a good job of keeping her mind off of everything else happening around them, that she had almost forgotten why he was really with her. Their lunch had seemed almost like a date with comfortable conversation and relaxed eye contact.

But it wasn't a date. They'd never go on a date.

Nate was inside her classroom at that moment checking to make sure that there was no one in there waiting to kill her.

She sighed and a frog lodged in the back of her throat. Her life would never be normal again. But did she want normal if Nate wasn't part of it?

"All clear," he announced, holding the door open for her. "I'm going to take a quick sweep around the perimeter of the building. I'll be right back. Don't leave this room until I come back." Then he disappeared. Again.

With a heavy heart and heavier footsteps, she set off for the cabinet with supplies for upcoming classes. She had a job to do regardless if Nate was in her classroom or her life. Andy should be back soon. He would bring some normalcy to her world. And if he was around at the shop, then maybe Nate wouldn't spend so much time so close. Maybe he could watch her from farther away with another man around.

Maybe she could wean herself off of Nate, so that when they parted ways it wouldn't be quite so hard. So her life wouldn't feel quite so empty.

She hated herself for growing so attached to him. When had he become so indispensable? When had just the thought of his ruffled brown hair and early morning beard started bringing a smile to her face?

Even now, she could not ignore the telltale skip of her heart as he opened the door. The sound of his footsteps sent her pulse skittering and brought a smile to her face.

"Back so soon?" she asked, her head still stuck in the cabinet. He didn't respond, so she stepped back to see what else had his attention.

But it wasn't Nate standing by the door.

It was Kirk Banner.

She stumbled back from the cabinet, as he took a step toward her. His eyes were cold, almost vacant, and his face looked almost emotionless. His nose twitched like he was going to scratch it, but he didn't lift a hand. It was then that she noticed that he held a large wrench, tapping it menacingly against the palm of the opposite hand. "I'm going to get what I need. Today."

She gulped, her mouth suddenly parchment dry. "What do you need?" she croaked.

A sneer transformed his face from that of a relaxed surfer dude to an ominous intruder. Below his unkempt curls his eyes turned hard. Almost evil.

Her gaze darted to the tool chest, but it was across the room, and there was nothing at hand to protect herself. Kirk blocked the path to the only exit, and there was no way she could defend herself against a larger man, especially an armed one. She thought about calling for help, but the building was built of reinforced walls to keep the sounds of the auto shop from disturbing the neighboring classrooms. They were probably empty already anyway.

And Nate, her protector? Well, he was probably on the other side of the building by now.

And here she was face-to-face to Goodwill's man.

She was going to die.

THIRTEEN

As Nate rounded the corner of the building, he spotted an unremarkable car parked three spots over from his own sedan. It hadn't been there before, but he knew he recognized it. He'd definitely seen it in this same lot before class one night.

The rest of the building was deserted, as far as he could tell, so whoever was in the building was inside with only one other person.

Danielle.

Sweat broke out on his forehead, and he sprinted toward the door at the end of the building as though racing for a prize. His feet pounded the ground, but it seemed to take forever for him to reach the entrance. Breaths coming quickly and shoulders rising and falling heavily, he yanked open the door and darted down the hallway passing one, two, three doors.

As he approached the fourth door, he skidded to a halt, sucking in air to control his breathing and silence his movements. The door was open just a crack, and he could hear Danielle speaking softly.

His immediate reaction was to burst through the door, start shooting and ask questions later. But that would just lead to a shootout and probably end with Danielle and the suspect getting shot. And spending too much time in his head was a surefire way to make a mistake that would bring that result.

He'd never be able to forgive himself if he let that happen.

He needed to be in control, needed to be strong right now. So he leaned toward the small opening and peered into the room. Danielle stood on the far side of the room, her hands held out, palms facing down in a submissive position. Her voice was low and soft.

"Please. What—" her voice broke, so she swallowed, took a deep breath and continued. "Whatever you need. We'll get it worked out."

He couldn't help but be proud. She was more soothing than some professional negotiators that he'd worked with. The pace and timbre of her words were spot-on. Suddenly he realized that instead of making a plan, he was busy admiring this amazing woman.

Admire later, Nate. Plan now.

"You're right, you're going to give me what I need." The vaguely familiar voice from the other person in the room was gravelly, not like he was an old man, but rather as though nerves were choking him. The ferocity with which he demanded whatever it was that he needed made him come across more desperate than in control.

Nate's stomach dropped to his knees. Was it possible that whoever was in the room with Danielle wasn't Goodwill's man? If that was the case, it changed the entire situation.

The man took a step toward Danielle, moving into Nate's line of sight. The other man wielded some sort of heavy tool, but a gun was nowhere to be seen. He leaned in menacingly, and Nate knew the time for planning had passed. It was time for action.

He slipped the handgun from beneath his sweater, silently turning off the safety.

"What is it? What do you want?" Danielle asked, her voice still calm and cool. Her eyes darted around the room, probably looking for some way to protect herself.

Holding his gun with a practiced grip, Nate toed the door open an inch at a time while silently praying for protection. *God, please keep Danielle safe. Help me to protect her now and to stay calm. Give me eyes to see and help me use good judgment.*

When he was fully inside the room, he cleared his throat softly. The other guy didn't notice, but Danielle's eyes met his across the room. Shock then hope transformed her face. Then something more than hope flowed between them. Or was he just hoping that's what he was seeing?

The other man glanced over his shoulder, then spun around, bringing him face-to-face with Kirk Banner. The other man's arrogance turned to bewilderment, and his face went slack for a moment, as he tried to put the pieces of the new situation together. The wrench in his hand stopped moving for several seconds, and Nate jumped at the chance to take control.

"Kirk, put down the wrench."

The other man looked at his hands, confusion filtering across his face, as though he didn't even remember that he held a weapon. But when he looked back up, the confusion was gone, replaced by anger. He swore violently before demanding, "Who are you?"

"You know me. I'm Nate Andersen." He longed to shoot a glance over Kirk's shoulder to get a read on Danielle, but he fought the urge, instead staying focused on the volatile man in front of him. "We're in Danielle's class together."

"But why do you have a gun?"

"I'm a special agent with the FBI."

"A special agent?" Kirk rolled the words around his tongue, and for the first time, Nate could tell that his speech was slurred, and the tip of his nose was pink. Kirk shrugged as if it didn't matter. "Who you looking for?"

"It doesn't matter. I'm here now, and I want to make sure no one gets hurt. So put down the wrench and kneel on the floor with your hands behind your head."

Nate knew the drill. He had to get even an unarmed perp into a submissive position before he could drop his guard enough to get him handcuffed. Kirk had had more than a little bit to drink, and the liquid courage made him unpredictable, which was dangerous for everyone involved.

Taking two subtle steps toward him, Nate closed the gap by half. Now he could almost smell the alcohol seeping from the man's every pore.

"Put it down," Nate said again, his voice quiet yet unyielding.

Suddenly Kirk's face broke, and tears leaked down his cheeks. The wrench hit the cement floor with a crash, and he spun around to face Danielle, who was watching the whole situation with rapt attention from the opposite side of the practice car.

"I just need an A," Kirk sobbed. "Don't you see? I just need to pass this class."

"Why?" Danielle didn't beat around the bush.

"They're going to kick me out of the program! I'm failing all of my engineering classes. My teachers hate me, and they're failing me. And if I don't get an A in this class, they're going to put me on academic probation and kick me out of school." He sniffled loudly. "I'll never get my degree. I'll end up serving fries and living in my parent's basement forever.

"I tried to change the grade book. I went to your home and looked for it, but it wasn't there. If it had been there, none of this would have been necessary."

"You're the one that broke into my house?" Danielle sounded borderline irate, but she kept her distance from him. "Did you break into the cabinet here in the classroom, too?"

Kirk managed a muffled sob and nodded his head quickly, falling to the floor in a heap. His slobbering mess inspired neither sympathy nor understanding. The kid was a jerk to everyone, and he didn't put any effort into this course. He probably didn't put much into any of his classes. Which was why he was failing.

Suddenly a twinge of compassion struck him as he approached Kirk's back. Nate had no idea what kind of life the kid had had. He reached out to grip Kirk's shoulder and offer a bit of encouragement.

Just as his hand touched the other man's gray T-shirt, Nate realized his mistake—he should have kicked the wrench out of reach.

The pain as the wrench connected with his thigh

made stars jump before Nate's eyes. He bit down on his lower lip to keep from screaming. He caught his finger just a fraction of an inch before it fully pulled the trigger, and blinked through the pain.

Leg throbbing and eyes watering, he tried to steady the gun in his hand.

In the instant that it took him to blink again, he heard Kirk scrambling toward the door. Nearly blind from the unwelcome tears, he quickly scanned the room. Danielle still stood by the far wall.

Knowing she was safe, he lunged for the other man, catching him around the ankles just before he reached the door. "Don't even think about it," Nate said as he pushed Kirk's head into the floor just enough to keep him there. He felt his back pocket for his handcuffs, but suddenly jingling metal caught his attention.

"Looking for these?" Danielle held his cuffs at arm's length.

Nate caught her eye and smiled, as he twisted the restraints into place. "Thanks."

Her smile was soft, and he had an intense urge to protect his own.

The thought slipped into his mind before he could control it. He liked the idea. They were good for each other. He dwelled on it for a few moments, consciously refusing to dismiss it like he always had before.

Dear Lord, I don't want to be like my dad and grandpa. I want to be a godly man. But I couldn't live with myself if I ever hurt Danielle.

"Will you call the campus police?" he asked, grasping at anything to get his mind into safer territory.

"Really? You want to call the police and get them involved?"

He gave her what he hoped was a reassuring smile. "Yes. Kirk's going to spend a little time in a place where they don't care if you have a degree or passed any of your college classes."

As Nate pulled Kirk to his feet, he cringed at the pain in his leg. "Thanks. You made this really easy not to feel sorry for you."

When they finally made it back to her home that night, Danielle wasn't sure she could walk from the car to the front door. Nate parked his car, got out and headed toward the door of her apartment. He was almost there before he looked around, probably just realizing that she hadn't followed him.

He looked at her through the windshield, and she just managed a slight shoulder shrug and a shake of her head. He smiled at her as he walked to her side of the car.

He opened the door and squatted to her level. A muscle in his jaw jumped and he squinted tightly for just a moment.

"Your leg?"

Quickly back in charge, he smiled. "Yeah, I'll just have a nice purple bruise from our friend Kirk. How about you? The adrenaline wearing off?"

"I guess."

His smile turned knowing as he tugged on her outstretched hand, kicking the car door closed behind them. She leaned her head on his shoulder as he unlocked her door, letting them into the apartment. At the couch, she fell into the fluffy cushions, and he sat next to her, wrapping his arm around her shoulders and tucking her into his side.

They were silent a long time before she spoke. "You're sure that Kirk wasn't Goodwill's man." It was a statement. She knew the truth, but she needed confirmation, just one more time.

"Yes."

"I thought… I was so sure, when he showed up. Ever since you told me who you are, I've just been waiting. I was so sure he was the one after me." She sighed, looking straight at a brownish plant sitting against the opposite wall without really seeing it.

"I know. I thought so, too. At first. But he wasn't a pro. He'd been drinking and was sloppy. He used a weapon that was handy. Professionals have their own and their favorites." She couldn't stop the shudder that coursed through her body.

He readjusted his arm around her so that she was so close she could feel the beat of his heart under her hand. It raced beneath her palm, and she suddenly understood. He'd been scared, too.

"The campus police checked his story with the registrar's office. They confirmed it. He was afraid of failing and being kicked out of school, so he was willing to do whatever it took."

They had spent several hours talking with the campus police officer who had arrested Kirk. Nate had gently yet quickly guided him to make some phone calls on their behalf. Officer Geisy had much easier access to school records and had confirmed everything that Kirk had spilled during his breakdown. The officer had then driven off with Kirk in the backseat of the patrol car to book him on charges of attempted assault.

"But why? It's not hard to pass a class like Auto 101," she said.

He shook his head, the stubble on his cheek catching the hair on the top of her head. "Fear and alcohol can make people do stupid things, I guess."

She didn't say a word, hoping he would go on.

"I don't personally know about alcohol, but I do know about the fear." He swallowed thickly. "Sometimes you just get so scared of doing the thing that you don't want to do. You're scared of being the man you despise. You try to ignore it.

You do everything you can to pretend like everything's okay, as if you're not worried all the time about doing the worst possible thing."

She tilted her head to get a good look at his face, but he seemed to be staring at the same brown plant that had caught her eye moments earlier. "What do you mean?"

He shook his head and looked almost surprised when he glanced down at her, almost like he'd forgotten he wasn't alone. He cleared his throat, his dark eyebrows pulling together. Eyes that were usually gentle and filled with concern were suddenly blank, like he was trying to keep her from seeing what was really going on in his mind.

She put her hand on his arm and twisted so they could look at each other more directly. "Nate, you can tell me. Anything."

His lips pulled up into a half-hearted smile like he didn't quite believe her.

"You can trust me. I trust you."

"Oh, yeah? Prove it." His grin turned a little bit wicked, and she was tempted to take the bait and let the conversation move into safer ground.

Instead she said, "I've never told anyone how much I miss my dad." She had to break eye contact because she could feel her emotions spiraling out of control, and she didn't want Nate to have to figure out how to deal with a basket case. "I loved my mom a lot, and when she died, I really missed her. But I was only a kid, and I could always go to my dad for comfort. He was there for me while I was growing up. It's hard for a man, especially someone who's as quiet and conservative as my dad, to talk to a hormonal teenager, but he was great." A little chuckle escaped as some particularly uncomfortable memories jumped to mind.

And then it was quiet. Nate's breathing was slow and measured as Danielle waited for him. Settled back into his side, she let her breaths match his rhythm and was almost lulled to sleep when he finally spoke.

"I'm glad that you and your dad were so close. It's not like that with me and my dad." He swallowed, and paused so long she wasn't sure he would continue. "You know what I said before about fear?"

"Mmm-hmm."

"Turning into him is my greatest fear."

"What do you mean?"

"Man, my family is messed up. The guys just keep passing along to their sons traditions that aren't worth passing on. It probably started before my grandpa, but he's the first one that I know about. He was married to my grandma until my dad was about ten. Then he left them to marry a younger woman he'd been having an affair with. He left her a couple years later for an even younger woman. He died when I was really young, but my dad hated the man. Funny thing was, he was just like him.

"He treated my mom terribly. I mean, I thought everything was fine when I was a kid. I just thought she was sad. It wasn't until I was in high school that I realized that even though he never left my mom, he'd had multiple affairs since they were first married."

Nate shifted a little, and Danielle followed his line of sight to a picture of a girl on the beach hanging on the far wall. "It's my greatest fear that I'll end up like them. Sure, I want to be respected, but I want to be worthy. I want to be an honorable man. But I've already proven that I can't get involved with a woman without hurting someone I care about. It's what we Andersens do."

His gaze dropped to meet hers as she twisted to look at his face. As though he could read in her eyes the question she couldn't bring herself to ask, he said, "I was in college and met a girl who was really fantastic. At the time I thought I could break the cycle, but when I told her that I wanted to pursue a serious relationship, I found out that her best friend Georgia was really interested in me." He tugged on the hair just above his temples and clenched his jaw.

"It was such a mess. Georgia and I were good friends. I really liked her a lot, but even with the best intentions I broke her heart. I asked my dad for advice, and he told me what I already knew. The men in my family break women's hearts." He sighed, finally turning away.

"Nate, listen to me. You are not your father. You are not your grandfather. You are an honorable man. Know how I know?" She didn't wait for him to answer. "Because every night you walk me to my door and instead of coming in you go to the front office. The men you've described would never respect a woman enough to protect her from wagging tongues while keeping her safe from whatever else is out there. You're a good man, Nate Andersen."

His eyes darted toward the door as his forehead wrinkled. The muscles in his neck tightened, and he offered only a slight jerk of his head. "But this is different."

"Really? How so?"

His eyes shot back to meet hers, but they stayed unreadable. "We're not romantically involved."

She twisted her hands in her lap, barely keeping them from lashing out at his ridiculous excuse.

"How you treat me is a testament to your character, to who you really are." She swallowed thickly, trying to keep her emotions in check. After another swallow, she knew that if she didn't lighten the mood, her emotions would get the better of her and she'd be no use in convincing him of his admirable qualities.

"Just look how nice you've been to me," she chuckled, "even when I was being completely stubborn about the safe house."

"But that could just be part of my job," he parried, a glimmer of humor in his eyes. "You will recall that I was less then pleased with your proposition to stay in Crescent City." His mock-formal tone made her giggle, so he continued. "What makes you think I'd be so gallant with a real date?"

The words hung in the air for several moments, and the planes on Nate's face turned just a bit harder, as though he just realized what he'd said. He's eyelids twitched, like he wanted to look away, but he didn't.

She longed for the conversation to end, for Nate to get up and leave. At the same time, she couldn't look away from him, as she knew she had the words to tell him the truth. Words she didn't even like admitting to herself. Taking a quick breath, she let it out in a rush. "It's been a long time since I could trust anyone. Once you get used to not doing it, it's hard to let someone in again. But I trust you."

Squeezing his hand that lay on his knee, she offered a gentle smile. "It's the truth. You're a trustworthy man. I know it, or I wouldn't feel—"

Her cheeks suddenly burned, and she pressed her hands to her cheeks. Why did she let her feelings rush out without thought? She'd almost blurted out how much she cared for him.

Nate grinned impishly. He turned to face her and gently tugged on her wrists to pull her hands from her face. Then he used one finger to tilt her chin up, sinking the other hand into her hair.

"You're turning red!" He laughed just before his lips covered hers.

Her head spun as he deepened the kiss, telling her that his feelings were definitely as strong as her own. He was gentle and considerate, but the electricity between them was undeniable. His arm slipped around her back and pulled her a little closer until their knees bumped.

It seemed the signal to pull back, but as soon as they separated, she missed the security in his contact. Leaning in again, she tried to show him how much she cared. How much she appreciated the man that he was. Just how honorable she thought he was.

This time Nate pulled back, putting his hands on her shoulders keeping her at arm's length. His eyebrows pulled together, and he looked a lot more serious than she felt.

"I know I started this," he admitted. "But I need to stop it, too. Being distracted can only end badly. Don't forget there's someone trying to find you. Someone who has no qualms about using brutal force. We have to be on our toes."

FOURTEEN

Shooting himself in the foot would have been more productive than what he'd done the night before. Nate despised that he'd let himself do it *again*. He'd taken one look at the vulnerability radiating from Danielle's face, and he'd given in and kissed her. Soundly.

Sure, he'd ended their kiss, but he also instigated it. Her sweet innocence and the embarrassed blush that covered her cheeks had sucked him in.

He was noticing a serious and disturbing trend about his time with her. His self-control was almost nil and his excuses were growing where she was concerned. His attraction was far beyond his control. One look into her chocolate-brown eyes— even if he knew they were just contacts—and he was lost.

But that was no way to accomplish his mission. He'd earned a reputation as a case-closer because he got the job done and stayed in control. Not because he found himself falling for every assignment. Of course, he'd never fallen for an assignment before.

Except maybe he was falling for this one.

But he was ruining her trust, hurting her by offering her the hope of a relationship with each kiss. He knew that their future was uncertain at best. And he respected Danielle far too much to keep leading her on, risking that her feelings might grow as strong as his.

So why was he doing it?

Nate gripped the steering wheel of his car as he drove back to the garage after catching a few hours of sleep at his apartment. He'd hardly slept at all in the shop's office the night before. He'd tossed and turned, unable to find a comfortable position, his mind racing to remember the details of the kiss they'd shared. He'd looked and felt like a grizzly bear when Gretchen arrived at seven forty-five that morning, and instead of facing Danielle, he'd sent her a text message to tell her everything was fine, and he'd be back in a couple of hours.

Like a coward.

Which he knew he was.

His knuckles turned white on the wheel, and he clenched his jaw. "God, why is it that I have no control over this attraction to Danielle? I'm pretty good at being in control here, and the last thing I want to do is hurt her. But You and I both know that I'm bound to mess up any relationship I'm in.

"I've never had feelings like this before. Feelings that I can't ignore or push to the side. I'm feeling so far out of control on this one."

He knew that God already knew the things in his heart, but sometimes he just wanted to say them aloud and admit the truth that ate at his gut.

All too soon, he was pulling into the parking lot at the garage. As he stepped out of the car, he heard the steady clanking of metal on metal behind the closed bay door. Gretchen sat behind the front desk and waved at him through the large windows on the front of the building. He waved and even managed to offer a modicum of a smile.

As he entered the office, he heard Danielle calling through the open door to Gretchen. "I just don't understand him. One minute, we're having a toe-curling kiss, and the next thing I know, he's out the door. He didn't even come to say 'good morning' today. He sent me a text message. Can you believe that?"

Nate caught Gretchen's eye and held one finger up to his lips. She looked uncertain for a moment then offered a quick nod of her head.

Danielle dropped something on the ground and it clattered before she continued. "I just don't know how to read him. I mean…it's not like we're dating. I don't think." Then as an afterthought, she added, "Not that I'd really know, seeing as how I've never really dated. But still. What on earth is he doing?"

"I don't know, sweetie," Gretchen called back. To Nate she sent a glare that demanded to know what exactly he was doing.

He'd be happy to tell her—to tell them both—if he had any idea himself. He hung his head, as ashamed of his actions as he could be.

"So you don't know how he feels. How do *you* feel?"

Gretchen's words made his head snap up just in time to catch her mischievous grin on the other side of the office. He responded with a halfhearted grin as they waited for Danielle to respond.

It was silent a long time before her soft voice carried from the large bay. "I used to think it didn't really matter. I… I wasn't in a good place for a relationship. In fact I've never really been in a serious relationship. I couldn't because of…well… because I couldn't. But for the first time since I moved here, I'm starting to wish things were different just so that part of my life would be, too."

Gretchen looked confused, but Nate understood completely. As long as Goodwill's threat loomed out there, Danielle couldn't afford to settle down to have a normal life and a normal relationship. But it was all coming to a head. He was sure they both felt the tension rising. Soon she would either be free to live a normal life or...

Well, he wasn't going to dwell on the alternative.

"As for Nate, he's a good man, a very good man. Even if he is confusing." She tried to sound firm, but he could hear in her voice a lilt of affection. He knew it well. He'd heard it in his own voice plenty of times.

And there it was, that flicker of hope in his chest was back again. Hope for what, he didn't know. He had nothing to offer her. But what if his legacy didn't have to be passed on? What if he could just be a husband and a father without following in his father's footsteps?

It was silent for several seconds, so he decided it was as good of a time as any to make his entrance known. He opened and closed the front door loudly then announced his arrival. "Good morning, Gretchen."

"Morning, Mr. Andersen." She offered him a conspiratorial smile before looking back at the paperwork sprawled across her desk.

"Is Danielle in the garage?"

"I'm in here!" Danielle called before he could even get his question all the way out.

As he entered the large bay, he saw only two blue-clad legs sticking out from under the hood of a large truck. Her toes didn't quite reach the floor as she rested on the engine, stretching to reach something on the far side of the engine block.

Her feet kicked slightly until she slid to the floor.

Standing in her blue coveralls, a socket wrench in her hand, a grease stain on her left cheek, she looked so much like she had that first morning they met. But now they were friends, closer than friends actually. And Nate had to physically fight himself not to reach out and wipe the oil slick from her face.

But he'd heard what she said, and he let his guard down just a bit.

"What time do you want to go to the class tonight?" he asked.

She broke their eye contact and looked down at the tool in her hands. "I promised Ivey that I'd meet her there an hour early for some extra practice. Do you want to get something to eat on our way over there?"

"Sure. That's a good idea." He glanced at his watch. They still had at least three hours before they had to go leave. "Do you need some help until then?"

She looked doubtful. "You're doing fine in class and everything, but I'm not sure you're ready to start fixing cars."

He laughed. "I meant something more along the lines of washing them."

"Okay." Her head tilted to the two sedans parked on the far side of the bay. "Both of those are done, but they could use a wash and you can vacuum out the insides. The vacuum is in the corner over there."

Nate nodded and set to work cleaning the interior of the first car. Every time he turned off the industrial Shop-Vac, he could hear Danielle singing softly under the hood of the pickup. Her voice was gentle and sweet as she sang several praise choruses from church the previous Sunday. He'd thought she seemed distracted during the service, but apparently the music had stuck with her.

They'd been working for nearly an hour without talking, when Nate decided it was time to broach the subject of Ridley.

"Danielle, do me a favor tonight?"

"Sure."

"Don't get too close to Ridley."

"You think he's the one?" Her mind moved quickly, syncing with his own.

Nate shrugged, then realized that she couldn't see him across the large room. "I don't know. But I don't think he's harmless, and he is our only suspect at this point. With Kirk out of the picture, I just don't know who else it could be."

"So what do you want me to do?"

"Just don't wind up alone with him. Keep your

eye on him and if he makes you feel uncomfortable, let me know."

"He always makes me uncomfortable," she sighed. "Ever since that night in the parking lot last week when you showed up. He gives me the jitters. But whether or not it's Ridley, I do feel like something bad is about to happen. Do you think Goodwill's man is closing in?"

How could he respond without scaring her? "Maybe. No matter what, we have to stay on our toes, especially when we're out in the open. So follow your gut instincts and stick close to me tonight."

She mumbled something that sounded like "as close as last night?" before diving back under the truck's hood.

When Danielle finally finished with the last car and looked at the clock, she let out a loud sigh. "We still have a little while before we have to leave for class," she said, turning toward Nate whose large frame rested against the last car that he had vacuumed.

"You have something in mind to fill the time?" he murmured, crossing his arms over his chest.

She twisted back toward the office, to make sure that Gretchen wasn't within hearing distance. "I was wondering if I could talk to my dad again."

"Something you need to talk to him about?"

"Yes," she said, blowing a wayward strand of hair out of her eye.

"Like…"

How could she tell him that she needed to talk to her dad about *him?* Whatever was happening between her and Nate was twisting her insides out, and the only person she could tell about it was her dad. No one in Crescent City knew her background, except Nate. And she sure wasn't ready to talk to *him* about this.

"Like I miss him. A lot. Like I just want to tell him that I love him. Like in case anything happens to me, I want him to know why I had to stay."

Nate squinted for a long second before offering a slow nod. Reaching into his back pocket, he pulled out his cell phone and quickly dialed the number. "It's Andersen. Will you connect me to the old man?" He paused for several seconds, and his eyes didn't leave hers. Danielle wanted to look away, but she couldn't seem to make her eyes listen to her brain. "Mr. James, it's Nate Andersen again. Yes, she's fine. Yes, sir. I'm taking care of her. She's right here. She'd like to speak with you."

Nate crossed the space between them in three quick steps, holding the phone out to her, but covering the mouth piece with his hand. "Why don't you head over to your apartment? I'll wait for you in the office."

"Thank you, Nate."

He nodded as she nearly sprinted through the office and around the building, the phone pressed firmly to her ear. "Daddy?"

"Nora James, what on earth were you thinking not coming straight back to Portland with Agent Andersen?"

She froze at the tone in his voice, falling back against the door to her apartment that she had just closed behind her. "Dad, I'm sorry. I just had to stay."

"Why would you think you'd be safer there than here? You're breaking my heart, kid."

Tears streamed down her cheeks and fell from her chin. "It's not about my safety."

"What? What's more important than your safety?"

She swallowed a hiccup as she sank to the floor. "Yours." The silence was nearly tangible, squeezing her heart. After several more seconds, she had to continue. "Please don't tell me I was stupid or impulsive. You've been dead for a year and a half—at least to me. What if I could have done something to protect you and didn't? How could I live with myself if I was too scared to—to—save your life this time? Please, don't be mad at me." The last words came in a deluge as she waited for him to respond.

He mumbled something, and her mind saw his familiar habit of running his hand over his face, muffling words of frustration. He'd done that often when she was a kid, and it reminded her that he was the same man.

"You don't have to be scared. You did the right thing in the alley. I told you to run, and you ran. You did just what you needed to. And you don't have to be afraid now, either. I'm safe, and there are FBI agents everywhere." A small chortle snuck into his last word, but she wasn't ready to laugh.

"But how can I not be? Every time I've ever loved someone they've been taken away from me. First Mom. Then you. Well, you know.…"

"Is there someone else that you're talking about?"

How did he know? Even from this distance and after all this time, he knew her too well to let her get away with a generic discussion.

"Who is it, honey?"

"It was just you and me for so long, and when I was on my own, I just couldn't risk getting hurt again. But I've never met anyone like Nate before. He's…well… He's amazing and so good to me. It's just that I can't put him in danger, either. It's not worth it to me."

"Nora, listen to me. I love you, and I'm sorry that I ever got mixed up with Goodwill and put you in this situation. But I'm afraid, too." He sighed deeply. "I'm afraid that you're going to miss out on

great things that God has for you because you're
too scared to let anyone into your life. Doesn't tha
scare you, too?"

Danielle had just finished setting up for class
later that afternoon when Ivey pranced through
the door.

"Hi, Danielle!" she greeted, her normal exuber-
ance filling the wide corners of the room. Ivey's
eyes darted to the corner where Nate sat reading
and Danielle thought she saw the other woman's
smile falter for an instant, but then it appeared at
its usual wattage.

"You seem excited." Ivey's smile was contagious, and Danielle felt her spirits lifting, despite
the frustration that Nate had caused.

"I am! I just know that I'm going to get it tonight
Everything's going to make sense." Her eyes again
darted to where Nate sat, this time they stayed on
him for several seconds before meeting Danielle's
gaze again. She didn't say anything, but she didn't
have to. Her raised eyebrows were enough.

"He asked if he could come in a little early,
too. He just hasn't had time to keep up with the
reading."

"Oh, sure," Ivey said. "No problem. It'll be great
It's going to click tonight. I can just feel it."

Almost fifty minutes later Danielle wasn't sure
it was ever going to click for the other woman.

She just couldn't grasp even the simple concepts of a combustion engine and how the various systems worked together to create a working car. She tried using the example of the body, how systems worked together yet each had a unique function, but Ivey looked as lost at the end of their time as she had at the beginning.

"I'm so sorry," she sighed. "I just thought for sure it would all make sense today. I hate to keep taking up your time, but could we try just one more time?"

"Sure." Danielle gave her a kind smile and reassuring pat on the shoulder. "It's going to be okay. Let's do next Thursday before class again."

Ivey's face fell a little bit. "I can't come in early on Thursday. Do you have time tomorrow?"

"Okay. I have a busy day so I'll probably start early, but you can come to the garage around two."

"Oh, thank you."

Just then Ivey's cell phone rang. "Excuse me. I better take this in the hallway," she said after looking at the screen. She hurried out the door leaving Danielle alone with Nate again.

"That woman has a mental block for cars. I understood everything you said perfectly. You're a good teacher." Nate winked at her as he stood from the farthest seat away and made his way toward her. "How'd you get into cars?"

Danielle glanced toward the door to make sure it had closed securely behind Ivey and they wouldn't be overheard. "Andy was the first person I met here in Crescent City, and he was looking for a temp receptionist while Gretchen was on maternity leave. I offered to help out, and Andy taught me about cars." She shrugged. "It was all pretty easy for me. How an engine worked, how the pieces fit together, it just all clicked. Then I just had to learn how each make and model was different."

He opened his mouth like he was going to say something, but suddenly the door wrenched open and two students walked in.

"Hey," the younger of the two guys greeted them.

"Hi, Frank," Nate said.

The room soon filled with students, and the clock on the wall said they had only a minute before Danielle should begin, but there were still three seats conspicuously empty. Kirk's chair, of course, wouldn't be filled again. He was out for good. But Ridley's slicked-back hair and arrogant smirk were absent, and Ivey hadn't come back into the room.

Poking her head out the door, she saw Ivey still on the phone. A quick glance and she confirmed that the rest of the hall was empty, so she jogged toward the woman's turned back.

"All right," Ivey said, her tone clipped and harsh,

ot at all what Danielle was used to. "I'll take care
f it. Yes, it'll be done by tomorrow. I've got it all
ined up. I'll call you when it's done."

She spun just as Danielle reached out to
ap her shoulder, offering a guilty smile for
avesdropping.

"Just stuff at home. My husband… Well, you
now how he can be since the separation," Ivey
ffered as she forced a smile. For the first time
er skin looked tight across her face. Deep lines
narred her forehead, and she looked genuinely
oncerned.

"If there's anything I can do."

Now her face relaxed. "Just give me another
hance to understand cars tomorrow. My husband
vill just ridicule me if I've wasted all this time and
noney on a class I can't even pass."

Danielle gave her an encouraging squeeze on
he arm as they joined the rest of the class. "Okay,
et's get started," she said as she reached the front
f the room. As she spun around she noticed that
Ridley had snuck in while she was in the hall with
vey. He sat and glared at her from his spot near
he back. His eyes were angry, his mouth drawn
nto a tight line.

She remembered Nate's warning to stay clear of
im and not let him get her alone. Was he really
Goodwill's guy?

She tried to focus on teaching for the next hour,

but when she finally let them go for a ten-minute break, she could still feel Ridley's gaze boring into her back. She couldn't stop the shiver that enveloped her from head to toe. Since the class began, he'd been staring at her with a gaze that seemed to say, "I'm coming for you."

At the break everyone filed out of the room to visit restrooms or the snack machines, but Danielle felt glued to her desk. Ridley didn't move from his seat, either. But Nate was there, too. He hadn't left. She needed him to be by her side as Ridley continued glaring at her.

She tried to call Nate with her eyes, but he kept his seat, not maintaining eye contact and acting as casual as usual.

Was he trying to gauge Ridley's interest, to see how far he would go? Was he using her as bait to see if he could get Ridley to strike?

Ridley's eyes shot to Nate then back to Danielle, a sneer twisting his face.

She tried to catch Nate's eye again, and took a few steps toward him, just needing to feel his strength. She realized her mistake too late. Her path would lead her right past Ridley's seat.

If she stopped or turned around, he'd know that he'd gotten to her. Maybe he was on the verge of beating her, but he hadn't won yet.

Lord, give me strength, she prayed silently before marching in the same direction she'd been heading. She sucked in a breath and held it as she approached Ridley. His eyes turned dark as she drew nearer, but he didn't move. He didn't look away or pretend that he wasn't watching her with an intensity meant to unnerve her.

As she passed him, she let out her breath and allowed herself a quiet sigh.

Suddenly her left wrist was caught in a vise— Ridley's hand engulfing her forearm. He tugged and she stumbled backward.

"Let's go out somewhere after class tonight." His voice was low and it held an edge of steel. "Just you and me."

Terror shot up her arm and she tried to yank it free. "No," was all she could manage.

Heat suddenly filled her right side, and she didn't have to turn around to know that Nate was standing next to her. "She said no." Nate's voice had a strength that Ridley's childish demands couldn't match.

He looked down at his own hand clasped around hers then back up into her face. She tried to keep her expression neutral, almost bored. She couldn't bear to let him see the fear and disgust at his touch that made her stomach roll.

Ridley sneered directly into her face before loosening his grip just enough so she could pull her hand free.

Immediately she turned into Nate's arms and let him guide her out of the room and into the deserted hallway.

FIFTEEN

The entire drive back to her apartment from the college, every time Danielle closed her eyes, she saw Ridley's face. "What do you think he meant by all of that?" She knew she didn't have to explain or expound on her worries. Nate's tightly pursed lips and wrinkled forehead spoke volumes about his own train of thought.

"I don't know." Frustration laced his tone. "You're sure he didn't hurt you."

Danielle rubbed her wrist again, trying to wipe off the memory of his clammy hand wrapped around it. "Yes. I'm fine?"

Well, physically she wasn't hurt. Emotionally was another question. When she'd returned to the classroom with Nate, Ridley had been gone, and he hadn't returned when she resumed teaching. But that didn't erase the evil glint in his eyes that was seared in her mind. Or the way her stomach had flipped when he'd grabbed her hand.

She'd thought that was the end. She'd been sure

that Goodwill's man had found his mark, and he meant to make his move right there in front of Nate.

Nate reached over and laid his hand on hers. "You were great tonight."

She managed a weak chuckle. "Very funny. I nearly lost it in the hallway. I think I scared some of the students."

He nodded slowly. "You were upset. I understand. But you held it together through the rest of the class. It was impressive."

Was he teasing her? A quick glance showed his face to be smooth and free from indicators that he was joking. But if he was serious, she didn't want to talk about it anymore. She didn't feel impressive—just determined to make it through this whole ordeal.

He cleared his throat and moved his hand back to the steering wheel. "I need to tell you something about Ridley. It's not good news, but it's not entirely bad either."

Her brows furrowed so tightly that a headache exploded across her forehead. "What is it?"

"He's not Goodwill's man."

"He's not?" She rubbed her head and leaned against the car door. "How do you know?"

Never taking his eyes off the road, Nate said, "Goodwill hired a professional. His man won't reveal himself until he knows he has you right where he wants you. There's definitely someone else out there. But we still need to stay on our toes around Ridley. He's angry and he looked ready to do some serious damage tonight."

"Doesn't he know that I have enough people after me?" she grumbled. "Why does he have to join the party?"

Nate shook his head. "With a man like that, it's hard to tell. My best guess is that it's plain old-fashioned pride. You've shot him down two or three times now. A girl saying no to a guy like that—with all that slick-backed hair and expensive clothes—could be a blow to his already damaged ego."

She inhaled, releasing the air slowly.

"Well, thanks. That was really encouraging. I feel extra safe now." She didn't even try to hide the sarcasm in her voice and was rewarded with a flash of white teeth reflected in the floodlight from the garage as they pulled up to her door in the empty parking lot.

"I guess I should have waited until we were safely inside to drop that one on you, huh?"

"Yes."

"Sorry." He reached out an arm like he was going to put it around her shoulders and pull her into a side hug, but he suddenly dropped it and looked away. He climbed out of the car quickly, and she had no choice but to follow him to her front door.

She slipped her key into the handle and turned the knob before realizing that it felt very loose. "Nate, I think…"

"What?"

"I don't know. The handle…it feels funny."

Suddenly he grabbed her arm, tugging her behind him and nudging the door open with his toe. With his other hand he reached beneath his jacket and pulled out his gun. "Stay behind me," he whispered. But the warning was redundant as his arm snaked around her waist, keeping her so close she could feel his body heat through the layers of clothing.

He flicked the light switch right inside the door, his body sweeping to face every corner. In steps that she was sure he measured to let her keep up, he walked toward her bedroom.

On tiptoe she peeked over his shoulder. Her bedroom door was only open a crack. "Wait!" she whispered. "I left it open. I left my door wide open."

"Get back in the car. Now." She shook her head against his back and felt the muscles there tighten. "Go back," he said more urgently. "Lock yourself in."

"I'm not leaving you," she managed around the lump in her throat that betrayed the fact that she wanted nothing more than to do what he commanded. With clumsy fingers she knotted fistfuls of his jacket into her grip.

He shook his head and let out an aggravated sigh.

Then his boot connected with the bedroom door, and he roared, "I know you're in there. Get out here, now!"

Nate wasn't even close to being surprised when, after some shuffling in the dark bedroom, Ridley emerged. While conceited and completely self-serving, he used those things to mask his own insecurities. Men like that were easy to control.

"Whoa! What's going on here? There's no need for that." Ridley's hands shot up in a position of surrender. He swore under his breath, his eyes never leaving the barrel of Nate's handgun.

"What's going on here?" Nate couldn't keep the contempt out of his voice. "What's going on here, is you broke into my friend's home. You waited for her in her bedroom and were planning to do what? Wait. Don't tell me. I don't want to know what kind of sick, twisted guy you are, but this is not okay." Against his back Danielle tried to break free from his hold on her waist. He could feel the anger radiating from her in waves.

"What? That's not it at all. She invited me

here. She told me to be here. Gave me a key and everything."

"I did not!" Danielle burst from behind him, hands on her hips, practically breathing fire. Her petite frame turned stiff, ready to pounce.

Ridley looked like he'd just swallowed his tongue as Danielle charged him. Apparently the stress of the looming threat, coupled with the ego-maniacal imbecile standing before them, was enough to make Danielle a little more than crazy. For an instant Nate was tempted to let her take a swing at the other man. With the fight raging inside her now, he guessed Ridley was no match for the spitfire.

Just before she reached him, Nate snatched her around the waist, hauling her back to his side. She was clawing at his arm, eyes still trained on Ridley. "Do what I say or I'll let her go, and then you'll have to tell the police what a girl did to you."

Ridley's eyes grew large, and his jaw dropped to his chest. "You wouldn't. Sh-she wouldn't."

"Don't tempt me." Nate's voice was deep and demanded no argument. He'd trained it to sound that way for just such situations. "As for her—" Nate nodded slightly in Danielle's direction "—she's having a rough couple of weeks. You don't want to mess with her."

Nate could see the progression of thoughts crossing Ridley's mind reflected on his face. He went from disbelief to uncertainty to straight-up fear.

"Fine. Fine. I'll do whatever you tell me to."

Nate smiled. "Good. Danielle, call the police."

"Hey! You didn't say anything about calling the cops."

"Shut your trap." Any trace of good humor disappeared and with it his patience for this fool. "You're going to get everything coming to you." He looked down at Danielle, his arm still wrapped around her. She'd stopped fighting him, but her eyes were squinted almost closed as she glared at her would-be attacker, lips pursed in anger. "Danielle, will you call the police?"

She was still for several seconds, then finally nodded. "Okay." He let her go, and she immediately went to the phone, picked up the receiver and dialed.

Ridley stayed still, disbelief on his face, but he was smart enough to stay silent. In fact no one said anything after Danielle made her phone call. They simply waited like statues. Ridley looked nervously at the gun that a glowering Nate pointed at his chest, while Danielle stood on the opposite side of the couch near the front door.

It seemed like hours before the sound of the sirens finally penetrated their silent stand off. Gravel outside crunched beneath a car, two doors slammed and then fists thumped into the door.

"Ms. Keating? It's the police," hollered a woman. "We received a call."

Danielle jumped at the almost simultaneous pounding on the door and call of her name, but she quickly recovered and turned to open the door.

"Officers," she greeted. She swept her hand into the room and two uniformed officers, a man and a woman, followed her lead. Spotting Nate and the weapon in his hand, they both reached for their own weapons.

"My name is Nate Andersen," he said quickly. "I'm a special agent with the FBI. My badge and ID are in my pocket. I'm going to pull it out to show you."

"Go ahead," the man said, his hand still on his own piece.

Nate pulled out the black-leather case and flipped it open. The woman walked forward to take a closer look and nodded to her partner. "Looks good. What's going on here?"

"This is my home," Danielle piped up. "Nate was just dropping me off and I noticed that my door handle had been tampered with. He came in first to check it out, and he found Ridley in my bedroom."

"You know this other guy?" the policeman said.

"Yes. I've been substitute teaching a course at the community college, and he's enrolled in it. He threatened me tonight when I said I wouldn't go out with him."

The woman with red hair walked toward Ridley, handcuffs in hand. "Turn around, and put your hands behind your back."

At first it looked like he was going to comply. He spun around, but then continued, doing a complete three-sixty. Suddenly he sprinted toward the front door, banging heavily into the female officer and shoving her to the floor. In a flash there was only one person between him and freedom. Danielle.

The male officer was running toward the door, but he was too far away and wouldn't make it there in time. "Don't let him get away!" he yelled.

Danielle jumped out of the way. Then, just as Ridley passed her, she stuck out one foot, catching his. He flew to the ground, grunting in pain as the wind was knocked out of him.

Danielle hopped on one foot, a smile on her face, as the two officers jumped on the fallen man, cuffing him and charging him with assaulting an officer and resisting arrest. They were reading him his rights as they escorted him to the back seat of the cruiser.

"I'll be right back to get your statement," the woman said to Danielle, who nodded. She looked about ready to sink into a puddle, and she still stood gingerly on her right foot.

"Did you hurt your foot?" Nate asked, as he

came alongside her, putting his arm around her back for stability.

"I think I twisted my ankle when I tripped him."

"Let's sit down then." He helped her to the couch, then jogged to the freezer and pulled out a bag of beans. "They're not peas, but they'll do," he said, as he laid them on her ankle. His joke earned him a smile just as the officers came back in. They sat in the chairs across from Nate and Danielle, offering reassuring smiles.

"Tell us what happened tonight."

Danielle obliged, going into detail about her first encounter with Ridley in the parking lot at the college the week before and the look on his face at church the previous Sunday. She explained how she felt creeped out by his watching her, and how he'd threatened her that night.

And she did it all without ever saying Goodwill's name.

She knew that if she brought Goodwill into this mess, it would become even harder to separate the good guys, the bad guys and the really bad guys.

A swell of pride filled his chest and he had to physically stop himself from hugging her close to his side.

"And what about you Special Agent Andersen? What brings you to Crescent City? You're a ways from your home office." Apparently Officer Henderson had read his ID closely.

"I'm just taking some continuing education courses at the college and visiting my friend Danielle."

"Mmm-hmm," the officer grunted. He didn't sound like he believed Nate, but the pair stood and moved toward the door. "Stay close to town in case we have other questions for you."

"Will do. Thank you officers," Nate said, as he closed and locked the door behind them. Returning to sit by Danielle on the couch, he let her put her head on his shoulder. They were silent for a long time.

"Can I get you anything?"

"I don't think so," she said. "I just feel so all over the place tonight. I was terrified. Then I was just so angry at him that I wanted to scream. This is going to sound crazy, but I was mad at him for not being the real person I should be afraid of. I was mad that he was trying to make me scared when I have plenty of that going on without his help." Her voice hardened. "I was mad that he was in my home, the place that's supposed to be safe. I was just mad, and then I couldn't even see straight. I wanted to tackle him."

"And now?"

"Now I just want to sleep. I'm so tired."

He glanced at his watch. "It's almost midnight.

No wonder you're so tired. I'll go. You get some rest."

"No. Please don't leave yet. Stay for a little while longer."

He was halfway up, but slowly lowered himself back to the couch at her plea.

"Okay. Just a bit." He wrapped his arm around her shoulder, and she snuggled into his embrace.

She exhaled, her head falling onto his shoulder once again, and her eyelids drooping slightly. "Is it always going to—" A yawn cracked her jaw, and she giggled. "Sorry."

"Is it always going to what?"

"I don't know. Be like this?"

Squeezing his eyes closed, he prayed he could dodge the bullet he knew she was asking, and the unacceptable answer he had to give. "I doubt it. Once we nail Goodwill's man, everything will calm down. I don't think there's anyone else out there looking to break into your house."

She offered a small chuckle while shaking her head. "That's not what I mean, and you know it."

His throat suddenly went dry, and he swallowed uncomfortably. But he didn't have a response. His history hadn't changed. Couldn't change. He still had nothing to offer her. And he had to tell her as much.

No matter how much he cared about her.

SIXTEEN

Beneath Danielle's cheek Nate's shoulder tensed, his muscles twitching slightly. She lifted her head and tried to swing around to face him, but his hand on her shoulder kept her from twisting fully.

"Nate? Is something wrong?"

He cleared his throat and opened his mouth, as though ready to speak. Like a fish he closed it without saying a word. Such unusual behavior from a normally confident man.

Silence hung heavily on them, as she finally shifted from his embrace and turned to meet his gaze. His eyes were clear, but she couldn't read his emotions in the dark gray depths. There wasn't even a hint of blue in them today, and it made the fair hairs on her arms stand on end.

Rubbing the bumpy flesh on her forearms, she finally broke eye contact, searching for something—anything—else to focus on.

"Danielle." His voice was soft, pleading, as he hooked his index finger beneath her chin. Lifting until their eyes locked again, he swallowed thickly again. "I'm sorry."

Dear, Lord. It was the only prayer she could manage before the ambiguous look in his eyes solidified, and her chin started an uncontrollable quiver. "You don't—I mean, you and I—there is no—"

And then she couldn't stay seated a moment longer. Her feet pounded the floor as she paced wall to wall, her apartment never feeling so small. Nate stood as well, shoving his hands into the pockets of his jeans. With hunched shoulders he looked smaller than usual.

And was that pain etched across his face?

"Danielle, I am sorry. I didn't mean for this to get so far out of hand. I thought I could make it so no one would get hurt. But I can't be who you want me to be. I have a history and a past that I refuse to repeat. I won't be my father or my grandfather."

"But you're not them!" Her voice rose and almost cracked before she clamped both hands over her mouth and turned her back on him. Tears sprang to her eyes, and she knuckled them away with clenched fists. He wasn't worth crying over. He wasn't.

Maybe if she kept telling herself that, it would make it true.

Father, we have something special. I know we do. Why won't he take a chance? Can't he see that

I'm scared, too? But I'm willing to try for a future together. I'd rather push through my fear than miss out on what You have for me. Why is he being so stubborn that he won't do the same? He's not his father! Why can't he see it?

Nate walked across the room, getting so close to her back that his breath stirred her hair. She longed to turn into his embrace and just have him hold her. But that could only make things worse.

"Danielle, I'd hurt you if we tried to pursue something between us. Don't you see? I'd only end up ruining whatever we could have had. There can't be an 'us.'"

Swallowing the sob that rose in her throat, she clenched her fists and turned to face him. Imploring with her eyes, she tried to convey every confidence she had in the two of them—every reason for them to stay together. He looked away, shaking his head, and she reached for his arm.

"Nate. Please. We can do this together. I know you want us to be together."

Something like hope flashed in his eyes for a split second before he shook his head. "No."

"Please—"

"No." Another curt shake and a small step back as he crossed his arms over his chest. "I don't want it. Whatever you thought this—" he pointed back and forth between them "—was, it's not. I'm sorry…but don't you get it? This is for your own good. I'm no good at relationships."

She just shook her head. "How would you know? You tried once in college, and it didn't work out. Why won't you try again?"

"I know my history."

"That's not *your* history!"

"Yes it is. My dad. My grandpa. It's all my history."

"But you could break the cycle. You don't have to live like they did. Aren't you willing to even try?"

"And risk hurting someone I genuinely care for?" He sighed, stabbing his fingers into his hair. "Danielle, I do like you. A lot. I don't want you to be upset. And I'd never want to hurt you the way that I inevitably would. I just—" He shrugged, his face pinched with pain.

She rubbed her eyes, pressing against the burning there, as she walked around the couch, needing a little more space. There had to be something she could say, something she could do to convince him of the truth.

Clearing her throat and taking a deep breath prepared her for her last try. "Don't you think that God would help you make a relationship successful?"

"Of course, I believe He would. If that was His plan for me. But it's not. I realized a long time ago that I'm supposed to be single for the rest of my life."

Her breath left her nearly as fast as it had at the moment of impact after her bike crash. Clinging to the back of the couch, she leaned over and tried to regain control.

She felt Nate make a step toward her and held up her hand to stop him before raising her eyes to meet his. "A long time ago? You knew a long time ago? That you'd be single forever."

He nodded, confusion covering his face. "Yes. Back in college. After everything with Georgia."

This man by words and actions had shown that he cared for her—made her believe they could have a future. She'd let him into her life—the first person she'd let see the real Nora since before that terrible night in the alley.

And like a coward he'd betrayed that promise and her trust. He'd never even thought about having a future with her. He'd led her on, letting her hope for the best, all the while never putting his own heart on the line.

Ire that she hadn't even known existed rose in her heart. She tried to tamp down the anger splintering her soul before realizing it could give her the strength to send him away.

"If that's how you want it, then I want you out of my house now," she said, her tone rigid, all trace of tears vanished.

"I'm sorry. It wasn't supposed to be like this."

"It's too late for apologies. I want you out. Get out now!" She pointed at the door, and he nodded, resolute as he walked to the door.

"Fine. But I'm going to be outside your door all night."

"I don't care what you do. I just don't ever want to see you again."

"God this all went so wrong. I have no idea what just happened here."

Nate sat in his car, leaning against the steering wheel and watching Danielle's door. There hadn't been any movement since she kicked him out of her house more than three hours before. The outside light still shone, but all of the lights behind the curtains and blinds were off. She was sitting in total darkness or laying in her bed, trying to sleep.

Maybe she could sleep, but he knew he wouldn't be able to rest for a long while.

"God, give me wisdom."

He'd been shooting spurts of prayer toward the roof of his car at irregular intervals since Danielle kicked him out. It seemed the only way to let go of bursts of steam that threatened to shoot out of his ears.

He'd thought that she wasn't getting as attached as he was. He'd thought they could stay friends and no one's heart would be risked. He'd thought... well, a lot of things.

Apparently none of them right.

"God, how did I end up messing up this situation so badly? I just don't understand. I was doing everything right."

Except for kissing her around just about every corner.

"Except for that," he grudgingly admitted. "But I was in control of the situation. I had it completely covered. Danielle was safe—*I* was safe—and we were so close to figuring out who's after her."

He could feel it deep in his gut. After years in the Bureau, he knew the instincts that kicked in right when a case was about to break. And this case was about to break.

And, of course, he was completely out of control of the whole situation. He was good at being in control. Good at solving cases, investigating leads, following tracks.

He was terrible at being idle. Terrible at not knowing what to do next. Terrible at not being in control. But that was exactly where he found himself.

The moon slid behind a cloud, laying a blanket over the outer edge of the parking lot where Danielle's light didn't reach. The wind stirred, and the dried leaves of fall rustled in haphazard circles.

He was antsy. He had to get up and do something.

Stepping into the brisk autumn air, he made a quick walk around the building's perimeter. It was completely dark on the other side of the building, the clouds blocking the light from even the strongest stars.

As he walked, his mind kept conjuring Danielle's face, her soft features and bouncing brown hair, but he couldn't think about her now. That mess was a distraction. One he hoped they could work out later. Right now was about the case. About protecting Danielle.

With a conscious effort, he brought the details of the case to the front of his mind, thinking through the little things that had fallen by the wayside during the last couple days of panic. Ridley and Kirk had both been suspects of sorts, but obviously neither of them was the Shadow. So who was it? Was it another man in Andy's auto class? Someone they'd bumped into at church? Someone from the Y?

He methodically thought through the men he'd come in contact with, dismissing each with either an alibi or lack of menace.

But suddenly his mind jumped to the weight of Danielle's foot in his hand the night before as he gently laid the frozen-veggie bag on her ankle. Her skin was soft and pale, and it brought to mind the first time he'd administered first aid to that same ankle after she'd been chased through the woods.

That day he'd run around his entire complex, looking for the man who chased her. But he'd only seen a woman.

Immediately another memory jumped to light. This time of the shoe prints on his deck. As he looked at them in his mind's eye, they were small-ish. Maybe too small for a man's. Could it be a woman's?

But how had he dismissed those clues?

He pounded his fist on his thigh, catching the corner of the bruise that Kirk had given him. He groaned in pain and disgust with himself.

Oh, Lord, I've been looking for a man, but it's a woman, isn't it? I've been distracted, worried about my feelings for Danielle, and I've missed the clues. I was so worried about being in control of this mission and my attraction to Danielle, that I overlooked the most obvious part of the assignment. Please forgive my arrogance and help me find the woman that's after Danielle.

His suspect had been sitting in front of him the whole time, and he'd failed to even recognize her.

On the backside of the building, he picked up his pace, hurrying toward Danielle's door. They had phone calls to make, and this wasn't about whether or not he'd misled her about their relationship. This was about her safety.

He was almost to the corner when the moon escaped from the protection of the clouds. Its light was already beginning to fade, dawn on its way. But it was enough to reflect off the metal barrel that materialized before him.

"Won't you ever leave?" asked a voice, sweet like chocolate and hard as iron. He knew it immediately. "I swear, everywhere I go, you're there. It's like you won't let Nora out of your sight for two minutes. Who are you?"

Nate opened his mouth to answer, unsure just how honest to be, but she didn't seem to really care.

"It doesn't matter. This ends now. She's mine."

He didn't hear the gun firing. He only felt a searing fire in his right arm before falling to the ground.

It sounded like a car backfiring right outside her window. Or a gunshot.

Danielle jumped from a sound sleep, glancing at her clock. It was just past five, and she hopped out of bed to investigate. Throwing a sweater over her pajamas as she tiptoed across the living room, she glanced at the lock on her front door. Still in place. Peeking through the blinds, she spied Nate's car sitting where he had parked it the night before. But he wasn't there to expand his academic horizons.

He was probably asleep in the office. Definitely. He wasn't in danger. She hadn't heard him moving around in the office last night like she usually did, but her mind had been filled with other things.

A twinge of concern plucked at her heart, and although she tried quickly dismissing it, her stomach rolled. He was a grown man. He could handle himself.

Except if that had been a gunshot.

If it had been a gunshot aimed at Nate, she needed to check it out. No matter how angry he had made her, she wouldn't run again. No matter how much her insides quaked at just the thought of going outside. She wouldn't turn her back at the first hint of danger as she had with her father.

But Nate wasn't her father. He'd taught her better than to run away, showed her how God had given her the strength to stand up for herself and the ones she loved.

"God, help me! I do love Nate," she sighed, running to her bedroom.

She wasn't the same woman, either. The one who had made a huge mistake, who bolted from the alley a year and a half before, was long gone, replaced by a woman who would never abandon someone she loved.

She threw on her coveralls, the first thing she

could find. Pulling her hair into a ponytail and shoving a couple pins in it to keep strays in place, she didn't even bother checking the mirror before running for the office. She closed and locked her door as she hurried around the side of the building toward the front door. Once inside she found no sign of Nate or his usual air mattress. Hands in her pockets, she spun around confused.

Where was he? Had he believed her the night before when she said she never wanted to see him again? She'd been angry. Hurt. Maybe overreacted a bit.

And what about his mission?

She backed into the garage, turning on the overhead light. Its brilliance compared to the barely there morning sun made her blink rapidly. When her eyes did finally adjust, her mind couldn't make sense of the woman standing before her, arms crossed defiantly across her chest. The woman's normally jovial expression had been replaced with a hard glare that made Danielle tremble.

"Ivey, what are you doing here? I thought we were getting together later today." As soon as the words left her lips, Danielle knew how foolish they sounded. "You're not here for an extra tutoring session are you?" Her hands shook violently, and she clasped them tightly in front of her, trying to keep the quaking from vibrating through her whole body.

Ivey smirked. "Aren't you the smart one? But et me tell you, you're not easy to get alone. Ever ince your bike accident, you've been stuck to Nate ike he was life support." Her smirk turned cruel. But don't worry. I took care of him earlier."

This was it. She was going to die in this moment, nd all she could do was pray for the forgiveness he knew she'd never get to ask Nate for.

SEVENTEEN

Nate's arm felt like it was going to fall off. O
maybe he was just wishing it would fall off.
hurt so badly that he figured not having an arn
would be better than the useless one dangling by
his side.

While running toward the front of the garage, he
risked another glance at the blood already begin
ning to crust around the hole in the front of his
arm. He knew there was a matching exit wound on
the other side. Ivey hadn't hit the bone and really
hadn't hit anything major. Just enough nerves to
make him want to crawl into the garage and die.

But he had to find Danielle.

Precious time had passed while he played dead
after being shot. And then he'd lost consciousness
at least once. But he didn't know for how long. Ivey
could have Danielle by now, and he had to hurry

"Thank You, God," he repeated over and over
his ears still ringing with the echo of the meta
Dumpster lid slamming down. It had happened

a split second before Ivey pulled the trigger. She must have jerked at the noise, sparing his life.

And the noise certainly woke Ivey's true target, which is why the hired hand had taken off before she checked to see that her aim was true. She probably thought he would be out long enough to make her getaway with Danielle.

"Thank You, God," he whispered once more as he looked at what really was just a scratch, knowing that God's hand of protection had been on him from the beginning. Eventually he would need to have it looked at by a doctor, but first he had to find Danielle.

Whatever it took to make sure that she was safe, he'd do it. Even if he knew his efforts weren't enough. He wasn't in control of this situation any more than every other one leading up to this moment. And for the first time, he recognized it.

Still running, he prayed silently. *Father, I know that You're hand is on this situation. I'd be a dead man without You. On our own, we're hopeless. Please protect both Danielle and I. We need You this morning.*

Nate stumbled on the step of cement leading into the office but collected himself before silently slipping into the office. The room was mostly dark, and he could see the light from the garage casting a small stream into the far corner of the room, where the door had been left ajar.

His steps were silent and his hand automatically reached for his weapon. But, of course, Ivey had taken it from him when she rifled through his pockets right after shooting him.

Unarmed and completely uncertain what his next step should be, he crept toward the door that stood ajar. A single voice echoed in the large bay and carried into the hallway. "You're coming with me!" Hearing the words coming from Ivey was at odds with everything that Nate had known about her. She'd perfected her cover as a middle-aged soccer mom, which made this paradigm shift even more unbelievable.

Plastic slid along plastic as she undoubtedly put a zip tie around Danielle's wrists. "Let's go."

"Where are we going?"

"You're needed in Portland. Right away. Mr. Goodwill's trial starts on Monday, and he plans to make sure that your father is convinced not to testify."

Nate heard their footsteps heading right to the spot where he was standing, and he had to make a quick decision. Should he duck and hide and let Ivey get on the road with Danielle, taking her who knew where? Or did he stay put and let Ivey see him? If he stayed put, then maybe Ivey would take him with them. Maybe he'd be by Danielle's side, wherever they went.

He almost laughed at how ridiculously easy the decision was to make.

When the door flung open, revealing Ivey and Danielle in silhouette, he tried to look broad and imposing. It wasn't as easy as it had been when he had two good arms and his weapon, but his true goal wasn't to intimidate Ivey. He just needed to get taken along to wherever she was going.

"I thought I took care of you," Ivey grumbled, pointing her weapon at his chest and dragging Danielle by the arm in her wake.

"Not good enough, I guess. Should have checked twice."

She huffed and waved the gun around like she was trying to decide what to do with him. "Fine. Have it your way." With surprisingly fast speed, she brought the butt of the gun up and slammed it into the side of his neck, sending him to his knees, wheezing for air. She moved quickly again, and before he knew it, his own handcuffs—the ones he'd taken from him earlier that morning—were wrapped around his wrists, cutting off circulation to his fingers.

"Walk. Both of you." She corralled them out the front door, quickly checking for passing cars or pedestrians.

He tried to catch Danielle's eye, but she looked straight ahead as they marched in the direction Ivey pointed. The only car in the parking lot was

Nate's, but Ivey had those keys, too. She popped the trunk from the remote and waved her gun into the compact space. "In."

Nate wasn't sure he would fit in, but did as he was told. A crazy lady with a gun wasn't someone he wanted to mess with, especially with Danielle in range. He stepped onto the industrial carpeting and slid down on his back, his knees practically jammed into his chest.

Danielle gave Ivey a wild look that Nate took to mean that she thought the other woman was as crazy as he did. But Ivey just pushed her in and closed the lid as they lay side by side in the tightest space he'd ever been in.

"Are you claustrophobic?" he said in a normal voice.

He felt her wiggle a little, rubbing against his good arm, and he was suddenly very thankful he'd crawled in first. "No. I don't think so."

"Good."

The car shifted as Ivey must have gotten in. She started the engine and the car trembled beneath them then skidded out of the parking lot, turning left onto the highway. They were heading away from town as Ivey began talking, probably on her cell. He could hear her speaking, but could not make out any of the words she was saying.

"We should be able to talk if we keep it down to a whisper," he said to Danielle.

"Okay," she replied, equally as quiet with a small lilt of panic in her tone. "What are we going to do?"

"I'm not sure yet. First—"

Suddenly Danielle sobbed loudly next to him. "I'm so sorry. This is all my fault. I didn't mean for any of this to happen."

He would have given everything he owned at that moment to be able to wipe those tears away. "Shh. Danielle, it's not your fault. Calm down, sweetie."

"But I was so angry. I didn't listen. I was just so sure… Why?"

"Why what?" Her mind had changed lanes faster than he could follow.

"Why did you come back for me? Why didn't you just follow Ivey and call for backup?"

"I wanted to call for backup, but there just wasn't time." He sighed heavily. "There's no way I was going to let you out of my sight for more than a second. What if I lost you? I'd never be able to live with myself if I let you get hurt. Or worse."

He heard her inhale deeply and swallow, but he cut her off before she could continue. "I want to talk to you about this—I really do. But first I've got to get out of these handcuffs."

"How?"

"I'm not sure. They're too tight for me to slip

out of them without dislocating my thumb. Do you have a hairpin or something like that?"

"Yes—in my *hair.* How am I supposed to reach it?"

He snorted. Good point. "Can you scoot down toward our feet, and I'll try to get my hands up to your hair to pull it out?"

Without a word she complied, and soon his fingers were running through her silky hair. For a moment he forgot about the screaming pain in his arm and the handcuffs cutting off his circulation and just enjoyed the softness of her locks.

But the feel of the edge of a pin yanked him back to the task at hand, and he tried to pull it free without being able to see it. He snorted as the pin wiggled out of her hair and he popped it into the tiny hole on his cuffs.

Bingo! The lock on the cuffs popped, and he pulled his arms from behind his back, rolling to his back and suddenly realizing he was laying on her arm. She didn't complain, but he slid as far toward the front of the car as he could.

"I don't have anything to cut the zip tie with. Are you doing okay?"

"How much longer will it be?"

He rubbed his sore shoulder. "I don't know. And I don't have a plan. Yet."

"We can kick out the taillights. They're designed

to pop out easily so that kidnapped kids can flag down help."

"But what if Ivey notices before someone else does? I'm sure her response would be less than pleasant."

A soft humming noise coming from Danielle's side of the trunk filled the quiet space before she suddenly whispered, "What about the release pulls on the back of the seat to make it fold forward? Most cars have them in the trunk now. Can you feel them?"

Nate groped along the upper edge of back of the seat until his fingers wrapped around a plastic tab. "Perfect—it's right here. Good thinking. I'll use it as soon as Ivey pulls over and gets out."

"Why do we have to wait?" He could hear her shifting uncomfortably. Her wrists and shoulders were undoubtedly killing her.

"We can't afford to have an accident where one or both of us are injured. If we surprise her while she's driving, we could wind up in a rollover accident. If we're injured, she's got the upper hand again. Worse, she might have time to signal Goodwill that something's gone wrong." He exhaled sharply. "If he gets more of his guys here before we can get back up, we'll be in even deeper trouble."

"So what's Plan B?" she asked.

"We have to surprise Ivey in a place where she won't be able to get him on the phone. Ideally that

will be when she pulls over at a gas station or res
stop."

Danielle was silent for several long seconds
"I guess that makes sense. But you haven't really
answered my earlier question. Why are you in thi
trunk with me? Is this about the case? I know you
don't want to fail on this assignment."

He thought he heard her voice break, and i
made him smile. She was beautiful when she le
herself be vulnerable. He wished he could see her
but had to let her tone speak for her now.

"No," he whispered. "That wasn't it at all.
mean, of course I don't want to fail this assign
ment, but that's not why I'm tucked into this trunk
with you."

"It's not?"

Suddenly the car slowed, and he put his finger to
his lips, forgetting she couldn't see his movements
"This could be our chance," he whispered.

"Will you be all right?" Her words felt like a
hand on his arm, warm and comforting.

"I'll be fine. Stay put until I come back for
you."

"You will come back for me, won't you?" Fear
laced every word, and he knew she was worried
for him. He rested his forehead against hers a.
the car bumped to a stop. He wanted so much to
see her face, to see the worry there and offer her
reassurance.

More than that, he wanted one final kiss.

There was no way of knowing if he'd ever have another chance to do so. He could feel her rapid breath on his chin, and he knew this was his chance.

But it was also his chance to prove to both her and himself that he was worthy of another kiss if the opportunity ever arose.

Pulling back, he knew that he'd do anything he could to make himself worth just one more. Maybe, just maybe, that one more might lead to another one, and another one. Maybe one every day for the rest of his life. And he knew she was worth fighting for. Worth doing whatever it took to never hurt her the way his father had hurt his mother.

Instead of stealing that last kiss, he cupped her cheek and brushed his thumb along her cheekbone. "Will you pray for me? I think I'm going to need it."

"I will."

At that moment, the engine turned off, and the driver's door opened and closed with a thud. Nate waited two seconds, then rolled onto his injured arm and yanked the release tab. Cracks of light filtered into the trunk as the seats popped forward, and he blinked against the pain in his eyes. Unable to wait for his vision to adjust, he rolled into the backseat, shooting Danielle what he hoped was a reassuring grin before slipping to the floor in front of the bench seat and pushing the back rests into place again.

He popped his head up to peek out the window. Perfect. They were at a rest stop, the only other vehicles in the area were two tractor trailers parked in the overnight lot. It seemed as if a lot had happened since he last slept, but it was still early morning, so there were few travelers on the roads. Maybe he could take Ivey down without attracting any unwanted attention.

He tried to plan how this was all going to work, but he had no idea what he was facing. A quick scan of the front seat showed no weapons. She probably had both his and her own with her.

And then through the windshield he saw her, walking back toward the car, a can of soda in one hand. Her other hand appeared to just be relaxing in her pocket, but he could make out the shape of the butt of a gun there also.

Well, the gun was inconsequential. He didn't have a choice. He had to act now or there might not be another chance.

Flinging open the back door, he lunged forward, sending up the only prayer he had time for. *God, please watch over me!*

If he had expected Ivey to look shocked, he would have been surprised. Her face was resolute and angry as she swung the gun from her pocket into her outstretched arm and fired it twice in his direction as he dropped to the ground, rolling toward her. His head told him to get away, but all of his training reminded him that if he let her get away now, he'd probably never find her again.

He crawled two steps, closing the distance between them to about fifteen feet. His ears rang with adrenaline, but he could see her mouth forming words that would have earned him a severe spanking as a child.

Ignoring it all, he pressed forward.

Reach and disarm her.

When she leaned left, he followed her direction. He kept bent at the waist, but never lost visual contact with her face as his feet pounded forward. She fired again, and he could feel the bullet graze his back. It stung for an instant then faded with all the other mayhem.

Don't get distracted.

Suddenly a third body appeared in his periphery, and for an instant Nate feared the worst. Danielle had gotten out of the car and was now in Ivey's sights.

He took his eyes off Ivey for less than a second, just long enough to confirm that the new addition was actually one of the truck drivers.

It was enough time for Ivey to point her gun, point blank at his chest. She pulled the trigger.

He waited for the explosion, for the debilitating

pain. It didn't come. The bullet had jammed, and she was frantically trying to pull his gun from where she'd tucked it in the waistband of her jeans.

"Thank you, Lord," was all he could manage, just as he slammed into her, knocking them both to ground. His biceps throbbed as she punched his wounded arm.

He'd never been in a brawl with a woman, but this one didn't fight fair. She tried a kick that would have sent him writhing on the ground if it had landed, but he dodged it just in time. Even with close to forty pounds on her, he struggled to subdue the scrappy woman. She tried another punch at his arm, but he knew that trick and shifted so she hit the muscles in his shoulder.

She still had a lot of fight left in her, so he grabbed her with one hand around the back of her neck, using his thumb and middle finger to apply pressure to the carotid artery in her neck.

Her eyes screamed hatred at him until they closed and she went limp. He didn't blame her—he was about to send her prison, probably for life.

Flipping her over, he used his handcuffs to secure her wrists, then hoisted her to a standing position.

The lone truck driver stood several yards back, his mouth hanging open, hands shoved into the front pockets of his jeans. Nate didn't bother offering more than a quick nod to the stunned man as he dragged Ivey back to the car, opening the door to the backseat and lying her across the seat. In the front seat, he grabbed his phone. While hunting for his ID and badge, he made calls to the local police and Heather, each just a few seconds. Just enough information to get the right people on their way.

He was just finishing up with Heather, as he popped open the trunk.

Danielle, eyes closed and feverishly mouthing a prayer, was a sight for his tired eyes.

"Danielle." She peeked one eye open just a crack.

"Nate!"

She seemed happy to see him, and he drank in her smile as he scooped her into his arms and set her on wobbly legs. She looked like a newborn colt using her legs for the first time, so he kept his hands on her arms to make sure she didn't fall as he released the restraints around her wrists.

"I'm so glad to see you. Are you okay? Where's Ivey? What happened?" Her questions didn't stop, they were just muffled, as she flung her arms around him and held on tight.

"I'm okay," he whispered over and over into her hair, brushing kisses across the crown of her head.

After several long minutes, she pulled back just

enough to look down at her left hand, which had been resting on his back. A crimson stain marred her soft skin. "You're hurt. We have to get you to a hospital."

"It's okay. Help is on the way."

As if they came when mentioned, sirens sounded in the distance, closing the gap to them in record time.

She seemed to know that their time alone together was coming to an end, so she hugged him once more, pressing her face into his neck. "Thank you." He wasn't sure if he heard the words so much as felt them.

And then the others arrived.

It was like bees swarming an especially potent flower. Paramedics, police officers and special agents buzzed about, patching up his wounds and pulling Danielle farther and farther away until he couldn't see her for the circle attending to her needs.

He didn't see her again that day.

He wasn't sure he'd ever see her again.

EIGHTEEN

Danielle's heart pounded in her throat when the judge told her to take the stand. She nearly tripped as her heels slid along the tiles of the courtroom floor, but she recovered with as much grace as she could muster. Straightening the line of her black pencil skirt, she squared her shoulders and marched toward the seat at the front of the room that the bailiff indicated.

She took the chair and waited for the U.S. attorney, Mr. Mortimer, to begin questioning her. He'd rehearsed the queries with her several times over the last week, but it wasn't helping the butterflies swarming her stomach. This was an important moment, and Mr. Mortimer had said he didn't want to take any chances. Hers was the testimony that could pound the nail in Goodwill's coffin—or so he'd said. Adding a young witness who had been kidnapped could only help, so he'd been eager to get her on the stand.

He was busy shuffling papers, taking his time

to see what reaction he could get out of Goodwill's attorneys. Her eyes darted to the other faces dotting the courtroom. It was almost empty, a closed courtroom, she'd been told. But there was one very familiar face, and as she met her father's gaze, she couldn't hold back a smile or the warmth that filled her chest.

His gold eyes, so similar to her own, stayed locked on her the same way she'd been unable to look away from him all week. If she looked away, he might disappear, and she would discover this was all a dream.

She was just learning how to blink again. Letting him disappear for a moment, and then realizing that he'd be there when her eyes opened. It was a lesson in trust that she could only master in time.

Eyes still trained on her dad, a small motion at the back of the room caught her attention. A man in a dark gray suit slipped out of the door, his movements silent and precise and somehow familiar. That brief glimpse reminded her of Nate.

But of course it wasn't him. Just a man with a similar build and hair color.

A quick glance around the room and she confirmed that he wasn't sitting in any of the seats. Had she really thought that Nate would show up? It was his case, but did she really expect him to be there?

Like every day since she'd last seen him, her heart broke a little bit.

Taking a deep breath, she sought eye contact with her dad one last time before the attorney took his place behind a podium and started by asking her name and her association with Parker James.

Just like they'd practiced, she repeated the words, trying not to sound rehearsed. The attorney led her through her original kidnapping in Portland. She relived the night her father was shot. And then she had to tell the whole room about her last two weeks in Crescent City. She revealed how Ivey—she had to get used to calling her Heidi Crane, the Shadow that had finally been identified—had gained her confidence, hunted her in the blue Explorer and chased her through the woods. And she told them all about Nate.

It was all so personal. Almost too intimate to share with strangers, especially ones that rubbed shoulders with him regularly.

But she had to talk about him.

As she told the story of running to his home after being run off the road, Danielle remembered the laughter they shared over a bag of peas. When she explained how Nate stuck by her side like a shadow for two weeks, never giving the hired assassin an opportunity to make a move, her mind wandered to their nightly ritual of him walking to her door then going to the garage's office. She couldn't forget those kisses either.

"Can you tell the court what happened on October 2 of this year, which was last Wednesday?" the U.S. attorney asked.

She swallowed and cleared her throat, hoping she could get through the story without breaking down. "A loud noise outside my window woke me up early, and I went to see if I could find Nate. He wasn't in his car, which I thought was strange, so I went into the front office. He wasn't there, so I went into the garage. I'd been giving Ivey Platt—I mean Heidi Crane—some extra tutoring for the class at the college, and I was expecting her later that day, but I was stunned to find her there so early."

It wouldn't help the case to admit that the real reason she'd gone looking for Nate was because of the fight they'd had the night before. How could she explain that that night and every night since she'd been plagued by guilt over her words and actions? She couldn't even put her finger on what it was that had caused her to react so emotionally, but she'd hurt Nate, and she needed to ask for his forgiveness.

And maybe with that forgiveness he'd offer her something more. Something that, if she was honest with herself, she'd hoped for since the first time he rescued her, the first time he kissed her.

Her hope had only grown with every minute they'd spent together and every selfless act on her behalf, the most amazing of which was putting himself in imminent danger so that Heidi would take him with them. He'd sacrificed his own safety, putting himself in front of the other woman's gun a second and even a third time even after he'd been shot.

It wasn't that she was in love with a hero. That just happened to be his job. What she longed for, what her heart ached for, was the laughter they shared, the compassion in his touch and the love in his eyes.

At least she thought she'd seen love in his gaze just before the paramedics had whisked him away. Maybe it had been something else, but she had to know for sure.

Oh, Father, I'm head over heels in love with Nate. You brought us together. You must have! And now I miss him so much. And I confess that I'm worried that he...that he...what? Doesn't love me at all? Was only feigning compassion at the rest stop? Thinks I've given up on him?

The sudden realization stole her breath, and she gasped loudly.

Mr. Mortimer stopped in the middle of the question he was asking. She hadn't heard a word of it, but he looked closely at her, a wrinkle marring his otherwise taut features.

"Ms. James, is everything all right?" asked the judge.

"Your honor, may we have a twenty-minute recess for my witness to collect herself?" the U.S. attorney asked. "These memories are quite trying."

The judge nodded slightly. "Twenty minutes."

Danielle barely heard the announcement, but she followed suit as the courtroom seemed to rise as one and all shuffled toward the door. *God, what if he doesn't know how I still feel? I have to tell him. Give me courage to tell him. I don't need independence. I don't need anything except You and him. Help me find him. Help me tell him. Please.*

Running across the slick floor as fast as her high heels and snug skirt would allow, she almost slid past her father but caught his arm just in time.

"Daddy, I love you."

"Are you all right?" he asked, wiping away a tear that splashed down her face.

"I am. I just…I just wanted you to know that I love you."

"I love you, too." His kind, dear face looked confused, and he squeezed her hands gently. "Are you sure everything's okay?"

She nodded. "It will be, but I need to talk to someone. To Nate."

"It's about time." Now it was her turn to be confused, and she must have looked it. "It's written all over your face every time you talk about him. You love him?"

She nodded. "With all my heart."

"Then go find him." He checked his watch. "You have eighteen minutes."

She smiled and gave him a peck on the cheek before racing toward the hallway.

Nate had been arguing with himself for more than half an hour. He knew he should go back into the courtroom, but he was a coward of the worst kind. He was afraid to face the woman he'd rejected—the woman he'd told he could never be the one. But he just didn't think he could survive listening to her recount their relationship event by event in cold, clinical terms.

If he heard her speak like that, he just might become convinced that she didn't remember that time with as much affection as he did.

And he wasn't sure that wouldn't send him right back to the hospital.

The sling strap around his neck itched, and he jumped up from the bench that he'd been occupying. He marched the length of the seat—all three feet of it—then spun and paced back. Running his good hand through his hair, he resisted the urge to pull it out by its roots. The arm that had been struck by the bullet ached badly, but it didn't even hold a candle to his heart.

How had he let Danielle just disappear that day at the rest stop? Why had he thought it would be for the best?

For that matter, why had he ever thought that not being with Danielle would be better than spending a lifetime with her?

He just wanted to protect her, to be by her side for the rest of their lives, but he'd been scared. So afraid of doing the same things his father and grandfather had done.

But he'd come to an understanding recently. As he watched all of his years of experience and training amount to nothing when he didn't figure out who Ivey was until it was far too late, he realized that he was human, prone to failure and not always in total control of the world around him.

God, I'm so glad that You are in control, and it doesn't have to be me. Thank You for rescuing Danielle and me.

God's strength and perfect timing had worked together to protect him and Danielle at his own weakest point, when his effort to protect them hadn't been enough. And why couldn't he count on that same strength to provide for him and protect his future marriage from the sins that had plagued the generations before him?

He knew the answer to that, too.

He could trust it.

His feet stopped pacing, and he let himself fall

back onto the wooden bench along the wall of the wide courthouse hallway. Men and women in business suits passed at brisk speeds, their hurried lives suddenly seeming far off as a sense of peace filled his chest.

Then his heart stopped.

Danielle stood before him, all beauty and class in her tailored outfit, her newly blond hair pulled back and eyes shining.

"I was hoping you'd be here." Her words were soft, but all other noise faded away as he stood, closing the gap between them.

"I'm sorry I didn't stay—in the courtroom, I mean." His words jumbled, and he clamped his lips closed to keep from saying more than he wanted to.

Her golden eyes roved his face, making the hairs on the back of his neck stand up like they had since the first time they met. Her gaze dropped to the sling around his neck, and she reached out and gently touched his forearm.

Concern made her voice husky. "Did you see a doctor?"

"Yes. She said that I'm fine now. I'm just not supposed to use it until the stitches come out. Something about how I might play too rough." He dismissed the idea with a shake of the head, but she nodded.

"Good idea."

They both laughed, and it broke the tension and uncertainty.

"I hear congratulations are in order. Your investigation has apparently brought down Goodwill's entire syndicate."

She'd been asking about him. She had to have been to hear that. It hadn't hit the media yet, and it certainly hadn't been announced that he was the one spearheading the entire investigation into the crime ring.

"Thank you. Goodwill's case is pretty much open and close, even if he hired the most expensive lawyers in the state. Between your testimony and your dad's and all of his men turning state's evidence and making plea bargains, Goodwill is going away for a long time." A flicker of emotion crossed his face. "And his cartel is crumbling around him. You and your dad are safe now. There's nothing for you to be afraid of."

She opened her mouth like she was going to speak, but snapped it shut. Her eyes lost their glow as she let out a slow breath between tight lips. Turning her head away from him, she watched the masses hurrying down the hall.

Danielle might not have had anything to fear, but Nate knew that he was dealing with a brand-new fear. The thought of spending the rest of his life without her was terrifying. And this moment was as good as any to tell her.

He tried to speak the words, tried to tell her how much he loved her, but the ache in the pit of his stomach that had always been associated with the idea of marriage didn't let go that easily. He swallowed and pushed it aside, trying again.

She beat him to it. "Listen, I only have five minutes before I have to be back on the witness stand, but I just have to tell you… I mean…" She looked frustrated with herself for not being able to finish the words.

There was no time to waste, so he sent up a quick prayer for courage and filled in for her, "I miss you."

She sighed and leaned in a little closer to him nodding. "Me, too."

"And I love you."

Tears filled her eyes, but her voice was clear. "Me, too."

Putting his arm around her back and pulling her closer until there were only inches between them, he whispered, "And I want to spend the rest of my life with you—even if you don't drink coffee."

She quirked an eyebrow, but didn't say anything. Instead she leaned in closer and pressed her lips to his. Her arms wound around his neck, and she held him so tightly that he wasn't sure if it was her hold or her kiss that made him struggle to catch his breath.

She was soft and pliant as he pulled her even

closer, savoring the taste of her berry lip gloss and relishing the knowledge that they'd have a lifetime of this.

"Ms. James?" called a male voice. They both turned without breaking their hold to see who was calling her. "Ms. James, they're about to begin," said the bailiff.

"I'll be right there." Then she turned back to Nate, a twinkle in her eye just for him as she locked her fingers with his and tugged him toward the room. "I guess I have to get this over with."

He held the large door open for her, and as she stepped past him, she leaned in for another quick kiss on his cheek. For his ears only, she said, "After I finish my testimony, I'd like to introduce you to my dad."

"But we've already met."

"I know." He'd read a word once used to describe the sunrise, and it jumped to his mind when she smiled in that moment—resplendent. "But I'd like to introduce you as the man I'm going to marry."

And for the first time he felt free. Free of the sin he had feared.

Free to love this woman for the rest of his life.

* * * * *

Dear Reader,

I'm thrilled that you've taken time out of your busy schedule to share this adventure with Nate, Danielle and me. Both Nate and Danielle struggle with fear throughout the story, and as I was writing the book, I spent a lot of time worrying about my own fears. But God was working in my heart, teaching me that He is still bigger than anything weighing on my heart.

My prayer is that, like Nate and Danielle, you'll discover that God is the One who conquers fear. When you face uncertainties, I hope that you'll turn to Him and see that His faithfulness never ends.

I love hearing from my readers. You can visit my Web site at www.lizjohnsonbooks.com or e-mail me at liz@lizjohnsonbooks.com. Thanks again for joining me on this adventure. I hope we have many more to come.

Liz Johnson

DISCUSSION QUESTIONS

1. Who is your favorite character? Why?

2. In the prologue, Danielle loses someone very close to her. Have you lost a loved one? How did you identify with Danielle's reaction to this loss? How was it different for you?

3. While we don't see too much of Andy, we know he's played a big role in Danielle's life. Who has been a caretaker, encourager, mentor and/ or friend like that to you?

4. Who in the story do you most identify with?

5. Early on in the story Danielle is a distraction to Nate, who thinks he has more important things to focus on. Of course, she turns out be who he should have been focused on the whole time. What things in your life started as distractions until you realized that God wanted you to focus on them?

6. Have you ever had something unexpectedly restored to you like Danielle's father is to her? What was your reaction?

7. Nate's father and grandfather have left him a legacy of sin that he feels certain he will

repeat. What legacies do you feel your family has passed to you? Are there positive traits that have been passed to you?

8. Danielle tries to tell Nate the truth—that he is not like his father or grandfather. But Nate isn't ready to hear it. Have you ever tried to tell someone a truth they weren't ready to hear? Has someone tried to tell you something you weren't prepared to hear? How did that turn out?

9. During Nate and Danielle's big fight about their future, whose side were you on? Why do you think you sided with him/her?

10. Do you identify with Nate's desire to be in control? Like Nate, have you reached a point where you realized that God has to be the One in charge? How has that changed your life?

11. Is there something that you're holding on to, refusing to give God control of? What's holding you back?

12. Most of us will never know what it's like to have an assassin chasing us, but we probably know what it's like to have other kinds of fear weighing us down. How has God made His presence known in your fears?

LARGER-PRINT BOOKS!

GET 2 FREE
LARGER-PRINT NOVELS
PLUS 2 FREE
MYSTERY GIFTS

Love Inspired®
SUSPENSE
RIVETING INSPIRATIONAL ROMANCE

Larger-print novels are now available...

YES! Please send me 2 FREE LARGER-PRINT Love Inspired® Suspense novels and my 2 FREE mystery gifts (gifts are worth about $10). After receiving them, if I don't wish to receive any more books, I can return the shipping statement marked "cancel." If I don't cancel, I will receive 4 brand-new novels every month and be billed just $4.74 per book in the U.S. or $5.24 per book in Canada. That's a saving of over 20% off the cover price. It's quite a bargain! Shipping and handling is just 50¢ per book.* I understand that accepting the 2 free books and gifts places me under no obligation to buy anything. I can always return a shipment and cancel at any time. Even if I never buy another book, the two free books and gifts are mine to keep forever.

110/310 IDN E7RD

Name	(PLEASE PRINT)	
Address		Apt. #
City	State/Prov.	Zip/Postal Code

Signature (if under 18, a parent or guardian must sign)

Mail to Steeple Hill Reader Service:
IN U.S.A.: P.O. Box 1867, Buffalo, NY 14240-1867
IN CANADA: P.O. Box 609, Fort Erie, Ontario L2A 5X3

Not valid for current subscribers to Love Inspired Suspense larger-print books.

**Are you a current subscriber to Love Inspired Suspense books
and want to receive the larger-print edition?
Call 1-800-873-8635 or visit www.morefreebooks.com.**

* Terms and prices subject to change without notice. Prices do not include applicable taxes. Sales tax applicable in N.Y. Canadian residents will be charged applicable provincial taxes and GST. Offer not valid in Quebec. This offer is limited to one order per household. All orders subject to approval. Credit or debit balances in a customer's account(s) may be offset by any other outstanding balance owed by or to the customer. Please allow 4 to 6 weeks for delivery. Offer available while quantities last.

Your Privacy: Steeple Hill Books is committed to protecting your privacy. Our Privacy Policy is available online at www.SteepleHill.com or upon request from the Reader Service. From time to time we make our lists of customers available to reputable third parties who may have a product or service of interest to you. If you would prefer we not share your name and address, please check here. ☐

Help us get it right—We strive for accurate, respectful and relevant communications. To clarify or modify your communication preferences, visit us at www.ReaderService.com/consumerchoice.

LISUSLP10R